KITTY
of Blossom Prairie

By Maurine Walpole Liles

Illustrated by Pat Finney

EAKIN PRESS ★ Austin, Texas

FIRST EDITION

Copyright © 1992
By Maurine Walpole Liles

Published in the United States of America
By Eakin Press
An Imprint of Sunbelt Media, Inc.
P.O. Drawer 90159 ★ Austin, TX 78709-0159

ISBN 0-89015-863-0

1   2   3   4   5   6   7   8   9

Library of Congress Cataloging-in-Publication Data

Kitty of Blossom Prairie / by Maurine Walpole Liles.
    p.   cm.
Summary: In the mid-1800s, twelve-year-old Kitty and her family demonstrate a pioneer spirit and bold courage as they struggle to create a homestead on the prairie in northeast Texas.
ISBN 0-89015-863-0 : $12.95
[1. Frontier and pioneer life — Texas — Fiction. 2. Texas — History — Fiction.] I. Title.
PZ7.L62695Ki   1992
[Fic]--dc20   92-17108
                                                                        CIP
                                                                        AC

To the memory of
Rebecca Walpole Garner
and her children.

Contents

Preface

Twelve-year-old Kitty Garner traveled 700 miles in an ox-drawn covered wagon from Tennessee to Texas in 1851. Her father had died earlier in Tennessee and her brave mother, Rebecca, thought that Kitty and her other five children would have a better life on the frontier in the new state of Texas. They crossed the Red River into Texas, where a trail led them to Blossom Prairie in Red River County, just fourteen miles south of the Indian Territory (now Oklahoma).

Kitty and her family demonstrate a pioneer spirit and bold courage as they struggle to create a homestead on the prairie. They fight Indians, weather a severe storm, lose their crops to heavy rains, and suffer from prairie fever (malaria). But they learn to love the wild, beautiful, flower-blanketed land in northeastern Texas.

Kitty Garner faces a dangerous adventure as she rides north into the Indian Territory to assist a wounded Texas hero, Big Foot Wallace, in delivering a vital message from Sam Houston to an Indian chief. The experience forces her to make some difficult decisions about the meaning of survival and the importance of happy childhood memories.

Author's Note:

The real Kitty Garner lived out her life on Blossom Prairie in northeastern Texas. She was a scholarly woman who remained unmarried but devoted to her family. Her nephew was John Nance Garner IV, former vice-president of the United States. She is remembered in his biographies as the family historian. She preserved old letters and fond family memories. Kitty is credited as the person who stimulated young John's interest in the pursuit of learning.

Kitty of Blossom Prairie is a historical fiction novel, but the events in the story could have happened, for there are records of Indian attacks, severe storms, floods, peddlers, and malaria on Blossom Prairie in the early and mid-1800s.

1.

The Indian Attack

Kitty woke to the sound of a rooster crowing. For a moment she thought she was still in Tennessee, until she opened her eyes and became aware of her surroundings. She was in the new log cabin on Blossom Prairie, and the family did not have a rooster. Her two younger sisters, Mary and Louisa, were already out of bed. She got up slowly, wondering if she was dreaming.

"It's a rooster crowing," Louisa called excitedly.

"We don't have a rooster," Mary mumbled, still sleepy.

"Let's go look," Louisa said as she raced toward the door.

Outside, the girls joined their mother, Rebecca, their older brother, William, and two younger brothers, John Nance and Charlie. They all stood near the chicken house, watching the rooster as he scratched the ground and crowed loudly. Cleaver, their small, shaggy dog, barked aggressively, but the rooster continued to crow. His feathers looked ruffled and dirty, as if he had been in a fight. The comb on his head was bleeding, and one wing

1

seemed to be injured. A strange rawhide band with a cord attached to it was on one leg. The rooster knew that there were hens in the chicken house, and he wanted to announce his arrival.

"Where did he come from, Mama?" the children asked.

"I'm not sure," their mother replied. "Perhaps he escaped from a wagon passing on the trail."

"He looks like a fighting cock," William said.

Rebecca shrugged her shoulders. "He may have an unsavory past, but we have twelve hens and no rooster. We need him, so I would say that he is God sent."

"Does that mean that we can keep him?" Charlie asked.

"We will unless someone claims him," Rebecca replied, watching the rooster with interest.

"What will we call him, Mama?" John Nance asked.

"He can crow as loud as Gabriel could blow his horn," Mary announced, and all of them laughed.

"Let's call him Gabriel!" Louisa shouted.

"Gabriel it is," their mother said happily.

As the rest of the family watched Gabriel, Kitty looked about the farm. She kept a journal and thought that she would like to describe the prairie as it looked at that very moment. Soft morning light was cast over the pleasant prairie land, and Kitty found it to be very beautiful. This was a gentle land in the Red River Valley, where large shade trees grew in the right places and pleasant streams ran lazily across the prairie. Some of the land had not been touched by the plow, and grass grew there tall and green. Deer, turkey, and prairie chickens fed and strolled among the trees in the nearby woods. The creek supplied plenty of fish.

Dotting the abundance of vegetation, bunches of flowers rose up from the grassy meadows, casting paintbrush colors and giving the land an almost celestial beauty. It was the profusion of flowers, capturing the eye and imagination of the early settlers, that caused the area to be known as Blossom Prairie.

Rebecca Garner and her six fatherless children had come from Tennessee and settled in northeastern Texas on Blossom Prairie in 1852. The family had only been in Texas a few months, but they had worked hard to develop a farm. They had built a cabin with help from kind neighbors, and planted vegetables and crops of cotton in the rich, dark soil.

Kitty heard Zona neighing in the corral, and she looked at the filly appreciatively. Her chestnut coat glistened brightly, and her mane was sleek and satiny. She had long, powerful legs, but there was a graceful tilt to her head. Kitty's uncle, John Walpole, had brought Zona from Tennessee shortly after the family arrived. She turned to see her mother watching Zona, and a happy expression crossed her face.

Rebecca often went to the corral just to look at Zona and pet her. When she was Kitty's age, Rebecca had owned Zona's grandmother, Ginger, and had raced her against Andrew Jackson's fine racing mare in Tennessee. Ginger had won that race. The children loved to hear Rebecca tell that story, and they knew that Zona reminded their mother of those carefree, childhood days on the family plantation. Kitty was proud that Zona had Ginger's blood lines. She delighted in riding Zona across the prairie as swift as an eagle. But most of all Kitty was glad that the mare gave her mother happy memories.

She gazed across the creek bank and watched the sun burst out hues of gold and orange on the eastern horizon. It felt good to soak in the beauty of the prairie and to see the flowers as they greeted the early spring morning. But as she watched the sunrise, the sky began to change in a strange way. Some of the colors looked like flames licking upward.

"Look!" Kitty called to her family, and pointed toward the horizon.

"Something's wrong, Mama!" William called in an

3

alarmed voice. The rest of the family turned around to look.

A thumping noise pierced the air and caused a change in the land. The calm and serenity of the morning seemed to be threatened. As the noise grew louder, everyone stood very still, waiting and listening.

"Horses are coming!" Kitty announced in a shrill voice. She felt a strong sense of impending danger, and William began to run toward the cabin.

Kitty saw the horses before they reached the creek, and William stepped out of the cabin with one of the Tennessee rifles.

Rebecca gasped. "Indians! Indians! Inside the cabin and bar the door!" she commanded. Kitty could sense the fear in her voice.

As the family rushed into the cabin, Cleaver followed on their heels. Gabriel fluffed out his wings and ran under the cabin.

Kitty watched from the window as ten riders crossed the creek and became clearly visible. They wore very little clothing, and their faces were painted with shades of yellow and red. Their long, black hair blew in the morning breeze. The Indians made strange yelping sounds as they rode swiftly toward the cabin.

"Indians . . . Indians are coming!" John Nance and Charlie yelled repeatedly.

William positioned himself at one window while Rebecca stood at the other. The rest of the family huddled near their mother as they waited for the Indians to make their move. They peeped through the window and watched as the riders circled the cabin several times, making their yelping sounds and striking fear in the hearts of the family. Kitty had heard some terrifying tales about Indian attacks, and she could not stop herself from trembling.

One of the braves rode closer to the cabin, and Kitty was startled to hear the loud, thundering sound of William's gun. The Indians then shot a flurry of arrows at

4

the cabin. William and Rebecca shot back at them with the rifles.

"Kitty," William called. "You and Mary must load the guns for us."

Kitty's heart thumped wildly as she moved to William's side of the cabin and began to load his guns. She watched as he rapidly shot at the Indians. It was as if she was somewhere else watching the fight. But she was right there in the midst of a battle, and they could all be killed.

"The rest of you children get to the center of the room and keep your heads down," their mother called sternly and fired the rifle. Kitty turned to see the fear on her younger brothers' faces. Rebecca watched their faces for a moment, too, and Kitty saw the sadness in her face.

The shooting continued. Two arrows made their way through the cabin window. One struck the kitchen table and lodged there.

Kitty loaded one of the guns and peeped out the window again. In the early morning light, the Indians looked like angry demons. William shot the gun, and one of them doubled over as the bullet found a target. Then the other Indians became very quiet as they took the reins of his horse and led it away from the cabin.

"They're going!" Rebecca called out. "Thank God, they're going!"

"They may be back, Mama," William cautioned her. "We must be ready for them."

They waited in silence for several minutes. Rebecca turned about to see how frightened her children were. John Nance and Charlie had begun to cry. Louisa, trying to soothe them, began to sing "Yankee Doodle." Soon all of the family joined her. The happy tune seemed to calm them while they waited for the Indians to make another move.

When fifteen minutes had passed, Rebecca spoke again. "Listen, children." Everyone was very quiet for

5

several minutes. "I don't hear anything, so perhaps they have gone."

No sooner had the words left her mouth before there was a loud noise and another attack started. This time two of the braves charged toward the corral for the horses, while the rest made a severe and determined onslaught on the cabin and its occupants. The sturdy log cabin had shielded the family from the numerous arrows that the Indians had plummeted toward them — until they brought forth a fiercer weapon. Now an arrow bearing a ball of fire sailed toward the cabin.

"It's going to be bad, Mama," William called between shots. "They aim to burn us out."

Kitty saw perspiration roll down her mother's pale, worried face as the Indians circled the cabin. They shot the flaming arrows on all sides, and yelled all the while. William and Rebecca repeatedly shot at them, and another Indian bent over. Kitty picked up some ammunition and looked through the window. The other Indians continued with their deadly task of trying to burn out the cabin's occupants. A fireball hit the table and Louisa screamed, making the ordeal even more terrifying.

"Girls," Rebecca called in a strained voice, "get the water bucket and put the fire out." Louisa and Mary obeyed.

"We're running out of ammunition," Kitty said quietly and looked about at the family she loved so dearly. She knew they couldn't hold out long, and she wondered what the Indians would do to them. She could only hope that they would not be killed.

"I'm out of ammunition," her mother said in a quiet, resigned voice. She began to gather her children about her in the middle of the room, but William continued to shoot at the Indians.

"It's no use, William," Rebecca said with downcast eyes. "The cabin will soon be on fire and we must get out."

William stopped firing and sat back against the

6

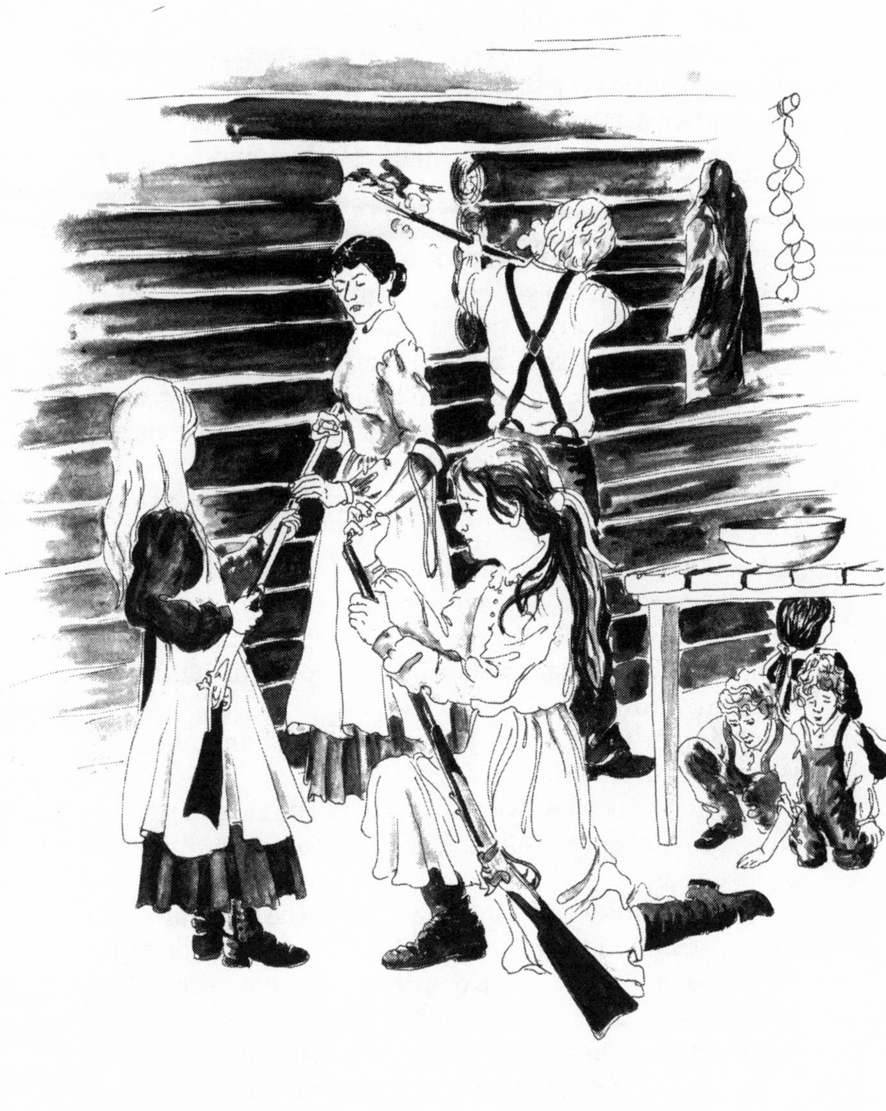

wall, while the Indians continued to circle the cabin. Kitty watched as her mother stood very straight and lifted her head high. Her facial expression began to change from worry to anger, and then to determination. Kitty knew that she was drawing on that special courage she had within her. All of them watched and waited for her to speak.

"We traveled seven hundred miles over the roughest, most hazardous trails known to man. We fought outlaws and wild animals to get here. All of us learned some hard lessons of survival on that trail, but we never once gave up. We claimed this rich prairie land as our home, erected this cabin, and planted crops. Well, we're going to hold it. I plan to stay, raise all of you children, and see you prosper. We were told to be ready to protect ourselves against Indian attacks, weren't we?" she questioned them firmly.

All of the children nodded.

Kitty watched her mother tilt her chin upwards as she continued. "We won't give in to these naked heathens. We'll fight them with all we can put our hands on," she boldly announced.

"Mama, we're down to two rounds of ammunition," William said solemnly.

"They will soon discover that, William, and come in after us," Rebecca replied. Then she began to direct her children.

"Kitty, take two flat irons from the fireplace and stand on that side of the door. Mary, take the top of the Dutch oven and stand next to her. William, stay where you are, and use your ammunition when the time seems right. Louisa, take the boys to that corner and stay with them. All of you must be very, very quiet," she commanded.

Kitty took the two flat irons from the fireplace. They were so hot, she had to use a towel to hold them. Then she stood by the door as her mother had directed.

Mary stood behind her with the Dutch oven lid,

8

while Rebecca stood on the other side of the door, holding the Dutch oven. Kitty's heart beat rapidly as they waited in a fearful silence for the Indians to come. All the time she silently prayed that they would go away and leave them alone.

Soon they heard someone kick at the cabin door. The girls jumped when they heard the loud crashing sound, then watched as the door fell in. Kitty and Mary were pressed very close to the wall as the Indian boldly stepped through the doorway. He saw William first and held his knife in preparation to fight. It was then that Gabriel crowed loudly and Cleaver grabbed the Indian's leg. The red man, startled and confused, hesitated. Rebecca took this opportunity to hit him over the head with the Dutch oven. The family watched in astonishment as he tumbled outside the door, making a great crashing noise.

His companions continued to circle the cabin, yelping and crying out as they rode. Rebecca motioned for the girls to resume their positions as another Indian came through the doorway. With black hair waving wildly, the Indian let out a blood-curdling whoop and sprang at Rebecca with a knife. Kitty trembled fearfully as he knocked the Dutch oven from her mother's hand. William shot the gun, and the Indian staggered outside with a bullet in his shoulder. Cleaver started to chase him, but John Nance caught the small dog.

They had little time to prepare themselves before another Indian entered with his knife drawn for action. William took aim at him but the bullet missed, giving the savage intruder a clear aim with his weapon. Just as he was about to throw his knife toward William, Kitty forced the hot irons into the middle of his back, causing him to cry out in pain. Before he could recover, Mary slammed the Dutch oven lid against his knee, forcing him to the floor. Rebecca recovered her Dutch oven and brought it against his jaw. Wounded and bleeding, he pulled himself outside to join the others.

The family got ready for another attack. They waited anxiously for several minutes, but the Indians did not appear.

"They've stopped yelling," Kitty said, and they all listened. Relief flooded their faces as they heard gun shots coming from across the creek.

"Tom!" William called out as he looked through the window. "It's Cousin Tom and some of the neighbors." He let out a deep breath of air. "They got here just in time too."

Kitty looked through the doorway and saw the Indians racing away from the farm, leading the Garner horses. "Zona!" she cried. "They've stolen Zona and William's horse."

"Quickly!" Rebecca called. "We must put this fire out, or the cabin will burn down. There's no time to waste."

All of the children helped to bring water from the creek. By the time the men returned to the cabin, the fire was out. It had not been burning long enough to do much damage. Kitty watched happily as the men led the Garner horses up to the cabin.

"Is everybody all right?" Tom asked.

"We're fine," William responded.

"They were Comanches," Tom said as he dismounted. "They were in a bad way too. Most of them were hardly able to sit a horse. What did you folks do to them?"

"We defended ourselves," Rebecca explained quietly. Kitty was very proud of her mother's courage and good sense.

"Looks like you did a good job of it," Tom said. "They turned your horses loose so they would have a better chance of getting across the Red River. There's been some trouble in the Nations, and a few Comanches are over there trying to stir up some of the young ones."

"I thought that the Comanches were farther southwest of here," Rebecca said.

10

"Some have been moving this way lately and visiting with the Indians in the Territory. Things bear watching right now, Rebecca," Tom said and looked north.

"I say we're in for an all-out Indian uprising," an old man on horseback called out. "Them red heathens aim to come streaming across that Red River and wipe us out," he added and spat tobacco on the ground.

Rebecca and the children looked fearfully toward the north.

"The civilized tribes in the Territory won't attack us, Gil," Tom explained. "They want peace as much as we do."

"Injuns are Injuns and they bound ta kill whites," the old man declared. "Why, as close as we are to the Indian Territory, we'd be the first to be hit. It will sure be a fearsome thing too."

The Garner family listened with concern as he continued, and Rebecca stepped closer to her children. The fear of the morning's attack was still with her. She knew little about Indians and believed that the old man could be right.

"You folks gonna be all right?" Tom asked, mounting his horse.

"We're out of ammunition," Rebecca informed him.

"I'll give you what I have in my saddlebag," he offered, then handed her the bag. "Best to keep a watch out till things settle down. We got other places to check."

"Mama, what will we do?" Louisa asked.

"We'll defend ourselves the best we can," Rebecca responded as she looked across the prairie.

As if he read her mind, William said thoughtfully, "This land is worth fighting for."

"We will survive and prosper here," Rebecca assured her family.

"We'll survive," Charlie repeated, in a small voice.

2.

The Peddler

The prairie was a lonely place, and the Garner family seldom had visitors. One fine spring day they stood in front of their cabin to welcome a traveler approaching. He rode in a cart pulled by a brown mule. Pots and pans, hanging from the sides of the cart, made a loud, jangling noise as the vehicle moved along. Other items, braced by tall side boards, were stacked high and covered by a patchwork quilt.

"Who is he?" Charlie asked.

"He looks like a peddler, son," Rebecca said as they watched him approach.

"What's a peddler?" John Nance asked.

"Peddlers sell things. This one probably sells cooking ware, and other household items," Rebecca explained.

"Will you buy anything, Mama?" Louisa asked.

"I could use some thread," Rebecca responded.

Kitty watched the man with interest. He was a very short man and had a long, uneven beard. He spat out a long stream of tobacco juice, and some of it spilled down his gray beard. His little brown eyes seemed to dart from

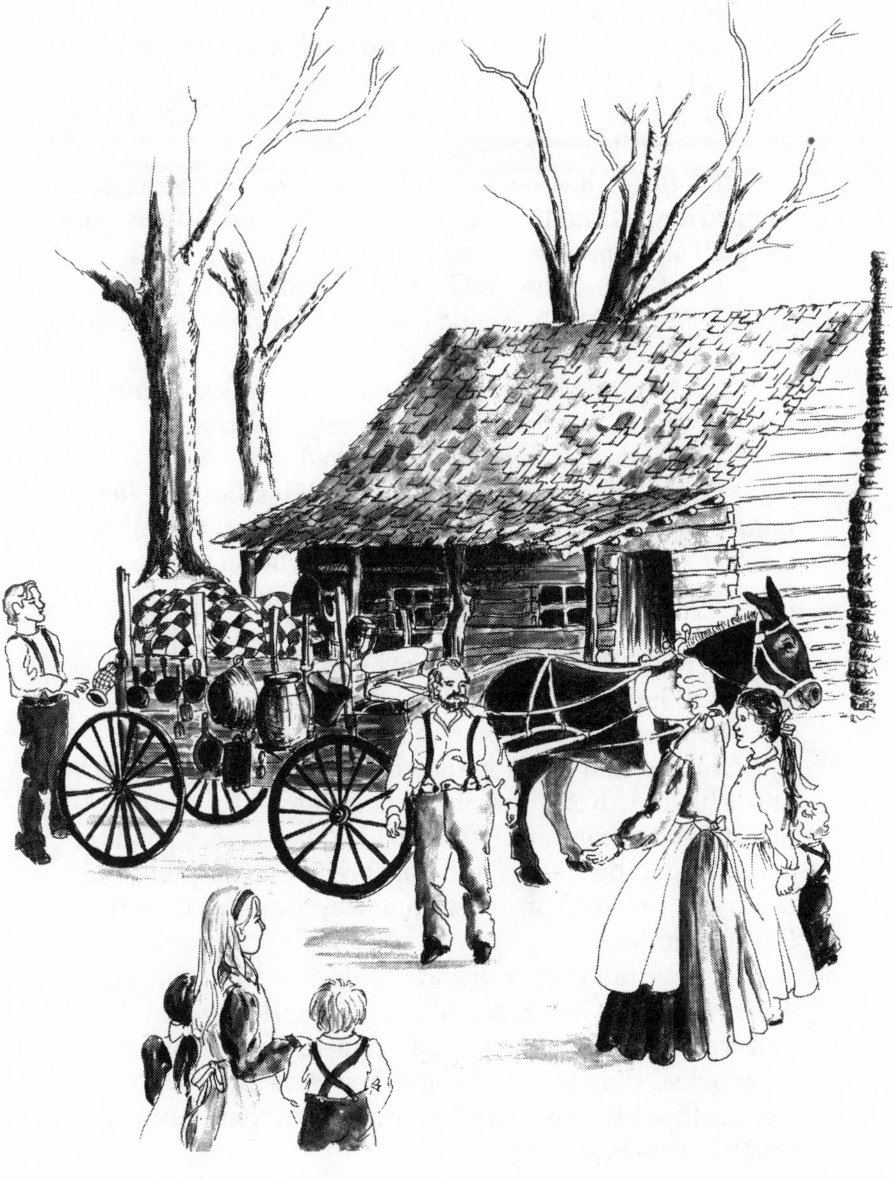

side to side, observing everything as he rode along.

"Do you think he'll have ammunition to sell, Mama?" William asked. "We need to have a good supply in case there's another Indian attack."

"We'll ask him," Rebecca said, and all of them waved at the man as he called a halt to his mule.

"Good day to you, sir," Rebecca called. "Won't you stop for a while and have a meal with us?"

"I'd take that right kindly, ma'am," he said and jumped down from the cart. "My name's Amos Juber." He gave all of them a warm smile.

"I am Mrs. Rebecca Garner and these are my children." The children stepped forward as Rebecca called their names.

"I'm mighty pleased ta meet all 'o ya. Missus Garner, that's a fine lookin' buncha young'ns ya got thar."

"Where do you live?" Louisa asked.

"Reckon I never had no home, Miss Louisa, least none I ever heard of. I was a orphan when I was about Charlie's age," he said, and patted Charlie on the head.

"We're having venison roast, cornbread, and some fresh vegetables, Mr. Juber. If you would like to wash up at the creek, William will show you the way. The girls and I will have the food on the table when you return."

"Sounds mighty good, ma'am," he said.

Charlie and John Nance darted after Amos Juber and William. Kitty watched them leave, then she followed her mother and sisters inside. They placed bowls of boiled vegetables and fresh cornbread on the table. Rebecca put the venison roast on a board and set it next to the vegetables.

As soon as they were all seated at the table, Mr. Juber began to serve his plate. The children watched, and waited to see what would happen. Their mother always asked the blessing before they were allowed to eat. She could see the surprised expression on their faces, and shook her head slightly.

"You must be very hungry, Mr. Juber," Rebecca said

14

kindly, "but if you will pause for a moment we will give thanks to God for our food. I will make it brief," she concluded.

"Yes, ma'am," he said, and eyed the food hungrily.

"God, we thank you for this bountiful meal. Amen."

As soon as Rebecca finished saying the blessing, the little man began to eat.

"Haven't had a meal since yesterday morning," he said between bites of food.

Rebecca began to pass dishes of food around the table, and the children served their plates with venison, turnip greens, potatoes, carrots, and cornbread.

"Didn't you have any food?" Louisa asked, and Rebecca gave her a warning glance.

"I had the grub, but didn't have no time to cook it. I been up in the Injun Territory," he explained between large bites of food. "There's some Comanches ridin' into the Choctaw Nation and even as far as the land of the Cherokees. Some 'o them young full-bloods in the Nations is gettin' a mite riled up over somethin'. Yes, sir, downright cantankerous, they was. Well, I seen how things was a rollin', so I jest high-tailed it back across that Red River. They ain't much fer traders anyhow, and jest let me into the Territory cause I lived with 'em and know 'em. I figger on moving toward Jefferson," he added and looked about the cabin.

"We were attacked by Indians last month, Mr. Juber," William informed him.

"I ain't surprised ta hear that," he said, and his eyes darted from one member of the family to the other. "Anybody hurt?"

"No, thank God, we were spared," Rebecca said.

"We'll survive," Charlie stated, and continued to eat his food.

"Do the Indians buy goods from you, Mr. Juber?" Kitty asked.

"Most always, I can make some good deals in the Territory," he responded.

15

"What kinds of goods do Indians buy?" Mary asked.

"They buy purty near the same wares that your ma here might buy, exceptin' medicines. They got no need fer white man's medicine, cause their own cures are better. The little people can come up with a cure fer most anything," he informed them.

All the children turned curious eyes toward Amos Juber.

"It's the little Injun people I'm talking about," he explained. "Ain't you never heard about the little Injun people?" he asked, and knew that he had captured their curiosity.

"Please tell us about these little people!" Kitty begged. The trader had fired her imagination with visions of little Indians.

"Why," he said with an air of importance, "they're a race 'o little Injun people that the medicine men call on fer cures when someone is sick. 'Course, most folks can't see them, jest medicine men and children . . ." The children listened and waited spellbound while he darted his little brown eyes about the room. "And a few other folks," he concluded.

"Now, Mr. Juber — " Rebecca started to protest.

"Oh, it's true Missus Garner. I swear, it's the pure truth. I seen two of 'em with my own eyes," he said, and looked at the children for a reaction.

"Leprechauns will show you the way to a pot of gold if you catch one, but they are far away in Ireland," John Nance announced, his blue eyes shining with excitement.

"Elves are mischievous, and they play pranks on people. They are far away too," Louisa informed them.

"The Lilliputians are just make-believe people," Mary said solemnly.

"We have never heard of the little Indian people, and they are only fourteen miles away in the Indian Territory. What do they do besides help medicine men, Mr. Juber?" Kitty asked.

16

"They help folks out when they're in need 'o help," he responded.

"I'm sure Mr. Juber has some other interesting things to tell about the Indians, children," Rebecca said sternly, while giving the man a warning look.

"Well, now, I reckon I have," he said and scratched his head as if he was trying to remember something. "There's them that's partial to religion. The missionary folks go in on a regular visit and some stay, preaching to the Injuns," he said, and looked at Rebecca for approval.

Rebecca got up and started to remove some of the dishes from the table, but the children remained seated with their attention fixed on Amos Juber.

"Tell us more," Kitty pleaded.

Mr. Juber nodded and began to talk of the Indians. "Some of the Injuns are sportin' folks," he explained. "They like to see a good cock fight or a horse race. I used to have me the best fightin' cock there ever was. Why, them Injuns would come from far and wide ta see my rooster, Texas Dancer, fight another cock."

"Where is he now?" John Nance asked.

"Lost him," Amos Juber explained. "Last month I rode along that old trail I jest come off of. I had me a load 'o goods to take into the Territory." He winked at Charlie and said, "I figgered on making me a tidy profit too. That's when I lost Texas Dancer. He rode right up in the cart with me, but somewhere along the trail he got loose and jumped out. I didn't miss him till I bedded down that night. Rode back a ways to look fer him, but didn't find hide nor feather. I figgered some animal caught him and et him whole."

"We have a good rooster," John Nance announced. "We named him Gabriel 'cause he can crow as loud as Gabriel could blow his horn."

"Is that so?" Amos Juber asked with interest.

"I'll show him to you," John Nance offered, and turned to his mother. "May we be excused, Mama?"

"Yes," she said, turning to Amos Juber. "Gabriel ap-

17

peared early one morning. We don't know where he came from, nor to whom he belongs. We were in need of a rooster, and he seemed to get along with the hens," she explained.

"I'd sure like to see him, Missus Garner. If it's the Dancer, your hens have been running with a high-class rooster," he said, and laughed loudly.

All of the family went outside to look for Gabriel. They soon heard the hens cackling and walked in that direction.

"Why, it's him fer sure!" Amos Juber said excitedly. "It's Texas Dancer! And me a figgerin' he was killed by a wild animal."

Gabriel did not pay any attention to the strange little man but continued to scratch the ground and call to the hens.

"Will you take Gabriel away, Mr. Juber?" Charlie asked quietly.

"He's a good fightin' cock, son," the man replied. "I been known to get some high stakes from his fights."

Kitty saw her mother tilt her chin up with indignation. "Gabriel will end up dead in the cock pits, Mr. Juber," she said. "He has a good home here, and a good chance to survive. I will trade you two good hens for him."

Amos Juber shook his head, scratched his beard, and said, "Nope."

"We have many vegetables, and a good supply of venison," Rebecca said as she attempted to bargain with him.

The man shook his head again and looked toward his cart.

"You may look about and see if there is something else that will make an equitable trade for Gabriel," Rebecca offered.

Amos Juber looked around the farm and then at the children's downcast faces. "I been offered good hard cash fer Texas Dancer, Missus Garner, but I never would sell him. I'm kinda partial to that ole rooster," he said, laughing. "Why, he kept me company on my long trips. When I'd take a nip from my jug, I'd pour some fer him —" He saw the frown cross Rebecca's face and stopped talking.

"Mr. Juber," Rebecca said sternly, "you know that whatever you get for that rooster will put you ahead."

"What's that you're saying, Missus Garner?"

"He won't stay with you," Rebecca explained, solemnly.

The little man looked at Rebecca as if she had discovered his secret.

"Gabriel would not be here if he had not run away, and you know very well that he will do it again," Rebecca concluded.

Amos Juber grinned and walked toward Gabriel. The children watched as Gabriel stepped between the hens and the peddler.

"Don't ya know me, boy?" Amos Juber called to the rooster.

"He's been here a whole month, Mr. Juber," Louisa explained. "I guess he has forgotten you."

"Might be the case, Miss Louisa. That jest might be the case," he said as he studied Gabriel carefully. "Missus Garner, I saw some fine looking bonnets inside your cabin hanging on pegs. If you could part with two of them, I'll leave Texas Dancer with you."

"It's a deal, Mr. Juber," Rebecca said happily. "Mary, will you get the two bonnets for Mr. Juber?"

"Yes, ma'am," Mary called, and ran into the cabin.

"Gabriel," Charlie called excitedly. "You're gonna stay with us forever!"

"It seems a waste of a good fightin' rooster, but I reckon that's the way of it," Amos Juber said, walking toward his cart.

The rest of the family followed him, and watched as he pulled the patchwork quilt back from his trade wares. They saw several Dutch ovens, kettles, pans, plates, and cups. Some fabric for dresses, men's trousers, a bag of

19

goose feathers for pillows, lye soap, and a small looking glass were also among the goods.

The children climbed up the cart wheels to observe all the items the peddler carried. Rebecca selected some thread and gingham fabric. William bought some ammunition. Then Amos Juber covered his trade ware up with the patchwork quilt.

"I want to thank you fer that good meal, Missus Garner. I also want to say that you're a purty good trader," he chuckled, and got onto the spring seat. As he picked up the reins, he looked toward the corral. "That's a mighty fine lookin' hoss ya got there," he said. "The Injuns know good hoss flesh and would prize her highly. She'd bring top price, Missus Garner."

"She's not for sale, Mr. Juber. I owned her grandmother when I was a girl in Tennessee, and Zona has the same blood lines. Our family will prosper here on this land, and live as we once did in North Carolina and Tennessee. Zona will produce good offspring for us," Rebecca informed him proudly, and added, "When you come this way again, stop in. We will be glad to have you take a meal with us."

"That's kindly of you, ma'am," he said, tipping his hat.

"Mr. Juber," Mary called to him, "did you really see the little Indian people?"

"I saw them, Miss Mary. Jest as shore as I'm a settin' here, I saw them," he said, and gave Rebecca a defiant look.

"Do you think they may come here?" Louisa asked.

"I reckon they might if you was to invite them," he responded, and rode away.

"The little Indian people will help us survive here," John Nance announced thoughtfully. "They'll help keep the mean Indians away too."

All of the children looked after Mr. Juber with wonder and excitement in their eyes.

"Children," Rebecca cautioned them, "you must not

20

believe everything that Mr. Juber says." The children did not seem to hear her.

"Someday I would like to go to the Indian Territory and see for myself," Kitty said.

"Me too," Mary agreed.

"I want to go too," Charlie, John Nance, and Lousia said in chorus.

3.

The Dark Wind

"**A**t last, it's finished," Rebecca said as she wiped her hands on her apron. The family stood back to admire the newly completed storm cellar. "It will protect us against storms and will also serve as a root cellar," she assured her family.

Kitty observed the structure closely. All of the family had worked on it in the evenings after the other farm chores were done. They dug a deep, rectangular hole near the cabin that was large enough for the whole family to stand in. Cut logs were notched on the ends and lowered into the hole. Then the family stacked the logs one upon the other, forming a vertical wall on the sides. William had hued out some logs to make shelves where vegetables and fruit would be stored. When that was done, they placed poles over the top. Dirt was packed over the poles to supply a roof. A small door at the top provided an entrance into the cellar, and steps were made of cut logs.

"Girls, I want you to place some candles, matches, and a keg of water in the cellar. If we have to wait out a long storm, we will have light and won't be thirsty," Rebecca instructed her daughters. "You will also need to place enough straw on the shelves to cover the potatoes, carrots, and turnips. When you have finished, I'll need all of you children to help pick more vegetables. We need to put away all the food we can, for it may be a long, hard winter."

"All right, Mama," Kitty said, and her sisters followed her into the cabin. As soon as the water, matches, candles, and straw were placed in the storm cellar, they joined their mother in the vegetable garden. The vegetable harvest had been good, and there was an abundance of ripe squash, potatoes, carrots, turnips, okra, beans, peas, gourds, and corn. The deer had taken note of the vegetables, too, and the family had surrounded the garden with a rail fence to keep them out.

When the children had picked a sufficient amount of vegetables, they took them to the front of the cabin to prepare them for the winter months ahead. The weather was warm, and Rebecca decided to work outside.

Several cut logs in front of the cabin provided good benches for the family to sit on, and they had moved the table outside to work on. Turnip greens, squash, and green beans would be eaten fresh, but some of the potatoes, carrots, onions, turnips, and dried beans would be saved. The girls cleaned all the dirt from the vegetables. Onions were tied, six to a large string, which hung from pegs in the cabin. Turnips were dipped in hot candle wax to seal in the moisture. Then large potatoes, long carrots, and waxy turnips were carried to the cellar. Those vegetables were placed on the newly made shelves and covered with fresh straw. Dried prairie grass was used for straw. The gourds were not eaten but were dried, cored out, and used for drinking cups.

John Nance and Charlie continued to pick vegetables while the girls helped their mother. Kitty noticed Rebecca watching them.

"Is something wrong, Mama?" Kitty asked.

"No, Kitty, I just wish that you children had more

time to play," she said thoughtfully, and added, "I'm
going to tell the boys that they can go fishing."

Kitty watched her mother walk toward the garden.
She, too, wished that they didn't have to work so hard
and had more time to play. But their survival depended
on hard work from all the family, even four-year-old
Charlie. She knew that her mother worked harder than
any of them, and Kitty felt sad. Rebecca had once worn
fine dresses and danced at colorful balls. Now she drove
oxen and plowed the fields.

Kitty heard Zona neigh from across the meadow. She
smiled. No matter how tired her mother seemed to be, she
could pet Zona and the weariness seemed to leave her.

The children had picked wild blackberries and plums
which grew along the creek bank. The plums had dried
on the roof top for a week and were now stored in cotton
sacks inside the cabin. Rebecca had made jelly and preserves from some of the fruit. There were so many blackberries, some were placed in crocks to cook later. These
crocks of berries were waiting to be turned into jelly and
preserves. Rebecca made a fire under her large washpot
and poured water into it. When the water had reached the
boiling point, she placed the empty jelly jars in the pot.
Over another fire she boiled some berries in an iron pot.

"The jars are clean, Mama. Why do you boil them?"
Mary asked.

"I'm not sure, Mary. I know that if they are not
boiled, the food will spoil," Rebecca responded. "Kitty,
would you get some more jars from the cabin?"

"Yes, ma'am," Kitty said and she walked into the
cabin. The jars were placed on a shelf in one corner.
When she approached the shelf, she noticed another
crock of blackberries. She removed the top and took the
crock outside.

"There is a crock of blackberries left, Mama," she
called.

"Oh!" Rebecca responded. "The storm cellar con-
sumed so much of our time, I forgot all about them. We'll

24

add them to this pot and make more blackberry preserves."

Kitty turned her nose away from the crock. "It doesn't smell very good, Mama, and there are bubbles on the top," she informed her.

"Let me see, Kitty," Rebecca said, looking into the crock. "They have gone bad and are no longer useful for jelly. Put the crock around the other side of the house, Kitty. We don't want it near enough to attract flies. I'll ask John Nance and Charlie to take it away from the house and pour the berries out."

Kitty did as she was instructed. She watched her mother lift the jars from the boiling water with a long prong and wipe them off with a cloth. She stood nearby and helped Rebecca ladle cooked berries into the jars, then the girls poured hot candle wax over it. The jars were placed on the table. Kitty knew that they would be placed in the storm cellar as soon as they were cool.

As Kitty worked, she looked toward the north and allowed her mind to wonder about the little Indians Mr. Juber had told them about. The thought of these little people just fourteen miles away was very exciting, and it offered the children many hours of interesting discussion. Kitty hoped that someday she could go to the Indian Territory and find out if they really existed. She thought she might even see some of them. But the people on Blossom Prairie did not visit the Indian Territory. They did not feel safe there.

It was late springtime and the prairie flowers still bloomed profusely. Kitty felt she had never seen anything so beautiful in her life. She wondered what the flowers did during the night while they waited for the morning sunlight to appear and warm them. But they must be here, even in the dark, and some eyes must be present to see and admire them, Kitty thought. The prairie seemed happy and peaceful at the moment. The birds were singing in the nearby trees, and there was the usual sound of insects fluttering from flower to flower. Kitty heard the hens cackling contentedly as they strolled about the yard with their chicks. But then she noticed that Gabriel was missing.

"Where is Gabriel?" Kitty asked.

"I don't know," her mother responded, and looked about her. "I wonder if that rooster ran off?" Before she could say more, they heard Gabriel let out a strange cackling noise. All of them stood still for a moment until they heard the noise again. Suddenly, Gabriel appeared before them, stretched his neck, and tried to crow. His beautiful plumage sparkled in the morning sunlight. But his head seemed to hang to one side, and his wings were drooped down in an odd way. He approached the log Kitty was sitting on and ruffled his wings as if he intended to fight it. Then he stumbled and fell. Rebecca and the girls watched him as he quickly righted himself, scratched the ground, and wobbled away.

"What's wrong with Gabriel?" Louisa asked as all of them watched curiously.

Rebecca did not answer immediately but gave Gabriel a suspicious look. "I knew that rooster had an unsavory past," she declared. "He must have become accustomed to strong drink."

"What do you mean, Mama?" Kitty asked.

"I believe that Gabriel is drunk on spoiled blackberry juice," Rebecca said. "We'll have to catch him and put him in the chicken house before he wanders off."

Kitty did not follow when her mother and sisters started after Gabriel, for there was something very strange happening to the land. The prairie provided the settlers with food, water, a place for their home, and much beauty. They knew its moods as a child knows its mother. It was vital to their survival that they learn to read the signs that spelled danger, and Kitty sensed that it was warning them now. The birds had stopped singing. The insects were very quiet, and the air had grown still as the prairie waited with an air of expectancy.

"Mama," Kitty called. "Something is wrong. It's be-

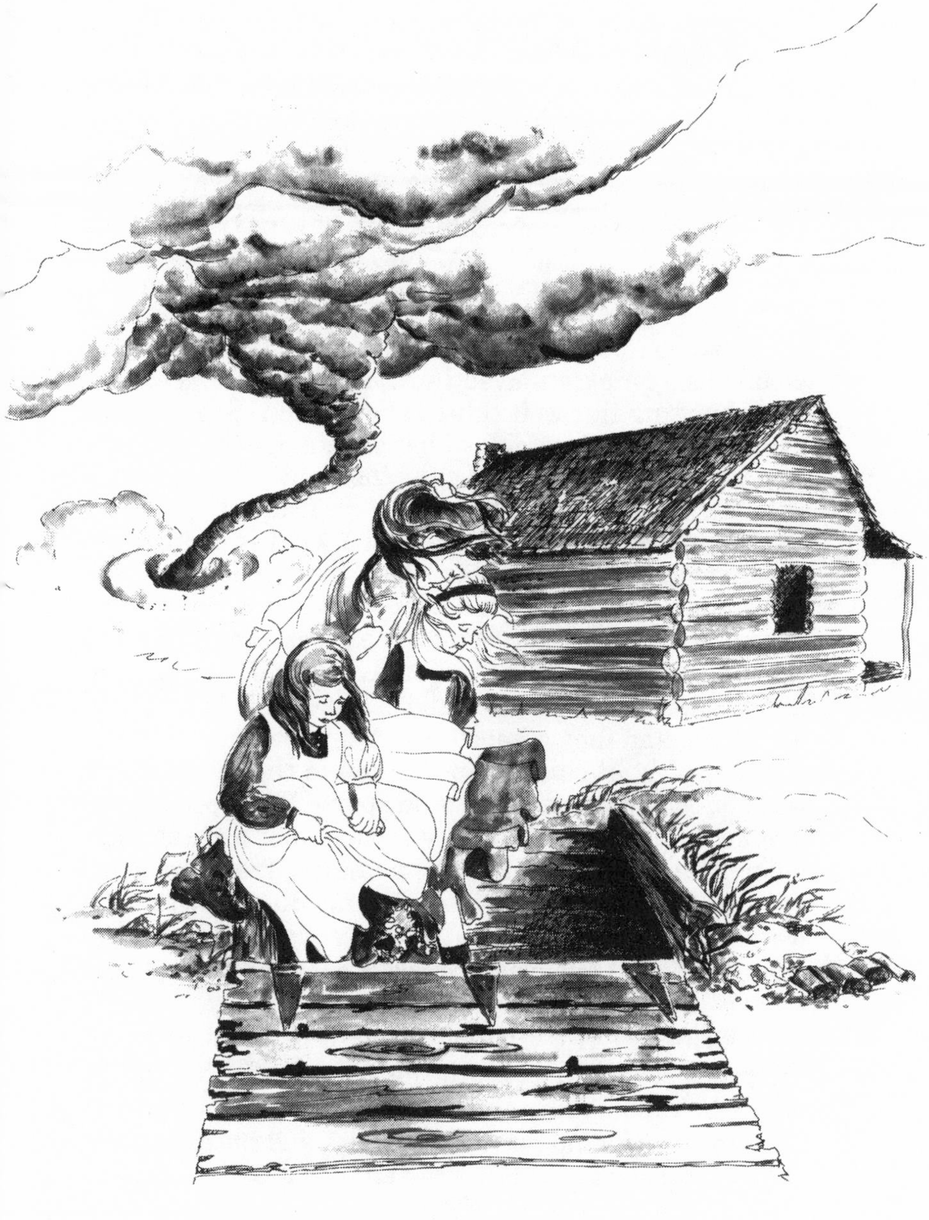

coming dark, and the chickens are going into their house."

Rebecca stopped and studied Kitty's expression, then looked up. As she observed the sky, and listened quietly, she gasped. "Oh, my God! William! William!" she called loudly. "Put the stock in the corral and run for the storm cellar. Girls, close the chicken house door and go to the cellar. Quickly, now, and don't come out for anything," she commanded them. "I'm going to the creek for the boys."

"What is it, Mama?" William called from the corral.

"It's a big storm. Now hurry!"

Kitty watched the sky for a moment. Dark, ominous clouds had quickly moved in over the prairie land and were hanging like evil things above them. She felt fear grip her heart as she helped her sisters put the chickens into the chicken house and close the door.

"Gabriel!" Mary called. "Where is Gabriel?"

"I don't see him, Mary, and the wind is picking up. We must get into the cellar," Kitty shouted and pulled her apron down as the wind whipped it about. She turned to see her mother approaching the creek. The wind was growing increasingly stronger. Kitty took her sisters' hands and headed for the cellar. Mary pulled the cellar door open, and they climbed in out of the wind.

The girls lit candles and waited in the cellar as the wind outside blew about in wild spurts. They peeped out through a crack in the doorway to watch as they anxiously waited for the rest of the family. The wind grew stronger by the moment, sweeping the dirt up with each whirl. Through the dust, Kitty saw William leave the corral and head toward the creek. Concern caught at her heart.

"William!" Kitty yelled through the gust of wind, "Mama told you to get into the cellar." She heard her words bounce about, and knew that William had not heard her. The wind howled with fury, and the girls grew more concerned about Rebecca and the boys.

28

"Why aren't Mama and the boys here?" Louisa asked in a small, frightened voice.

"I don't know," Kitty answered.

"Kitty, I'm afraid," Mary said. "What can we do?"

"Mama and the boys should be here by now. It may be that they couldn't find their way," Kitty answered. "We must go after them."

"Mama told us to stay here, Kitty," Mary cautioned her.

"Mama isn't here. She is out there somewhere with the boys, and she may need help," Kitty said. "We must think of a way to help them."

Mary lifted the door slightly and turned to the other girls. "Look out there," she called to them. "That wind would blow us away!"

Kitty waited for a few moments, straining her eyes to scan the area in front of them. The wind was even stronger now. She saw the washpot blow over, emptying its contents. A small tree was lifted from the ground, and the limbs were whirled into the cabin doorway. Some of the roof shingles were sailing through the air. Lightning was traveling across the sky in flashing red streaks. But there was no sign of the rest of the family. She rubbed her eyes and looked again, but she could no longer see the horses, oxen, and cow.

Kitty put the door down and looked about the cellar until her eyes fell upon a rope that lay on a shelf. "I have an idea," she announced, and her sisters looked at her anxiously. They watched as she picked up the rope and tied it to some of the logs which provided a wall in the cellar. Then she began to tie one end of the rope about her waist. Mary and Louisa watched silently, realizing what she had in mind.

"Mary, you and Louisa hold this end of the rope and pull me back in when I yank on it. When I get to the surface, I'll look for Mama and the boys," Kitty instructed her sisters.

"No, Kitty!" Louisa cried. "Don't go out there. Please don't go out there. You'll be killed!"

"I must, Louisa! I must!" Kitty told her, and climbed to the surface.

The wind was so strong that she could not stand up. She pressed her body against the ground and began to crawl forward, feeling the security of the rope as she went. She scanned the area as she moved, searching for her mother and brothers. The wind was whirling in great, loud spurts, and the sky was a sinister dark color. Intermittent streaks of lightning flashed across the ground as she moved forward, sliding her hand along the rope. Dirt and flying debris cut into her skin, and she was pulled about by the wind. But she tightly gripped the rope and moved on. Then she lay as still as she could, put her hands over her eyes, and peeped through her fingers to scan the area. A twisted streak of lightning shot across the sky, and hope flooded Kitty as she saw several vague images in front of her. Through the wind and dust she could make out the forms of her mother and William.

Kitty, clutching the rope, lay silently on the ground and studied them. Her heart leaped in her chest, and she felt as if her breathing would stop. Her mother and William lay very still on the ground in front of her, but John Nance and Charlie were not in sight. A large tree trunk stretched across the ground beside her mother, and fear struck at Kitty. Tears began to stream down her cheeks, and she prayed that they had not been hit by the tree — that they were somehow still alive.

In the loud and furious wind, Kitty began to crawl forward toward the still bodies. She saw her mother move slightly. Hope gave her more energy, and she moved closer to them. Happy tears struck her eyes when she saw that her mother and William were lying over the smaller boys, protecting them from the wind and flying debris.

"Mama," Kitty called as loudly as she could. "Crawl toward me. I have a rope to help guide us to the storm cellar."

The wind picked up her words and carried them far

30

away. She knew that they had not heard her. Suddenly, Kitty's eyes followed a thin strip of lightning across the ground very near her. A limb thrashed over her body and jerked the rope from her hand. Terrified, she turned about, searching for the rope and for her family. Fighting panic, she crawled over the ground, feeling on all sides of her. Then she felt a gentle nudge, and someone placed the rope in her hand.

"Mary!" she gasped. Mary pointed at William and Rebecca. Kitty saw William looking toward them and realized that they had seen her. Slowly, they began to move in the direction of the girls, pulling the younger boys with them.

Mary and Kitty remained still and waited while the wind whipped them about. It seemed to take their mother and brothers a very long time to reach them. Finally, William caught Kitty's hand and she placed it onto the rope. Mary did the same for Rebecca and they began to move along it toward the storm cellar.

When they reached the cellar door, Rebecca pushed the smaller boys inside, then waited until Mary, Kitty, and William were safe inside before she climbed in. It was a great relief to pull the door shut and close out the sound of the angry wind.

Kitty hugged Mary and said, "That was a very, very brave thing you did, Mary."

"Didn't you see the little Indian people, Kitty?" John Nance asked anxiously. "Mr. Juber said that they would help people who were in need."

"No," Kitty answered. "Mary helped me."

"The little Indian people are in the Indian Territory," Louisa informed him. "Mr. Juber said that we would have to invite them to come here before they can help us."

"Children," Rebecca told them. "It's very unlikely that the little Indian people ever existed. We should thank God that we're all safe." It was then that Cleaver

31

barked and John Nance pulled him from inside his shirt. "I'm glad you're safe too," she called to the small dog.

"That dark wind almost blew us away," Charlie declared, and all of them laughed.

"The wind wasn't dark, Charlie. The sky was dark," Mary informed him.

"It was," Charlie declared. "I saw it, and it was black and dark."

"The sky did look black," Rebecca assured him. "It will soon be over and we can go inside the cabin."

"I hope the cabin is still standing, Mama," William said.

The wind was dying down. No one spoke for several minutes, then William opened the cellar door slightly. "It's over," he announced.

A strange quietness filled the air as the family climbed out of the storm cellar. The storm had certainly brought a change to their farm. Shingles were missing from the roof, trees were uprooted, the rail fence around the garden was down, and much debris littered the yard.

Rebecca observed all of the damage and said quietly, "We can repair the fences and the cabin. What's important is that we are all here, safe and together."

Suddenly, a strange cackling sound emerged from the woods. Louisa giggled and called out, "It's Gabriel, and it sounds like he survived the storm too."

They watched as he walked out of the woods and stumbled toward them, trying to crow as he moved. They heard the cow, Suli, moo and saw the horses and oxen run about the corral.

"Well, children," Rebecca called to them, "we have work to do."

4.

Prairie Fever

It was just becoming daylight and the farm seemed to emerge from a shadow as Kitty walked toward the chicken house. She looked out over the land, and a concerned expression crossed her face. A few months earlier, the land had shown much promise with lush green cotton plants and corn stalks growing in the fields. But the end of summer came and Blossom Prairie was deluged by heavy rains for a week. Too much rain was as bad as too little rain. The cotton plants had been washed from the ground, and some of the corn had been destroyed as well. There would be no cotton harvest, and no money for the year's provisions. They needed those provisions and seeds for next year's crops.

At times the prairie was very lonely, and Kitty would walk off by herself and write in her journal. Today she carried it under her arm. She had recorded the Indian attack, Mr. Juber's visit, and the storm. She had also written something about the little Indian people. Now, despite the hardships it had brought, Kitty wanted to describe the prairie as it looked in the early morning light.

At the chicken house she unlatched the door and watched Gabriel emerge. He scratched the ground and strutted forward with a proud air about him. The hens followed.

"It's high time you hens were off the roost and scratching out worms for those chicks," Kitty told them.

She looked up to watch a bird fly overhead, and her face grew tense with concern. She observed the gray cast to its wide wings and the sharp, hooked beak. "A chicken hawk!" she yelled, shaking a finger at the bird. "Go away, Mr. Hawk! You may be sizing up your breakfast right now."

Gabriel, aware of the hawk's presence, ruffled his colored feathers, crowed loudly, and scratched the ground. The hawk took note of him and surveyed the farm once more. Kitty watched as the bird circled around and flew about in the trees. Then he stealthily approached the area where Gabriel proudly strutted about with the hens and chicks. The hens squawked loudly and Gabriel began to crow his alarm. He stretched his neck up high and displayed his multicolored feathers. Cleaver participated by barking.

Kitty watched the flock of chickens flutter about in fright and confusion. She looked toward the house for help as the hawk swooped down on them. She knew that her mother and William had heard the chickens squawking and Cleaver barking. William was always very good about protecting the animals, and Kitty wondered why he didn't appear with the gun as he usually did.

The hawk continued to circle low, eyeing the chicks greedily. "Go away! Leave those chickens alone!" Kitty yelled at him, but he paid no attention.

Everything happened very fast after that. Gabriel put on his battle posture, scratched the ground, and crowed loudly as the hawk swooped down toward a wayward chick. The rooster fluttered his wings vigorously and ran between the hawk and the chick. With his red-combed head waving boldly and his colorful feathers ruffled for battle, he warned the hawk to go away. The hawk didn't heed his warning, so Gabriel extended his wings and flew above the intruder. The spurs on the back of his leg were protruding outward as he hovered above the hawk. Quickly, without warning, Gabriel struck at the hawk and forced his spurs into its neck. The hawk's hooked beak shot out toward Gabriel, but the rooster settled to the ground and side-stepped him. With lightning speed, he spread his wings again for another attack.

The hawk was surprised by the fierceness of the game rooster. Wounded and bleeding, and with no desire for more, he quickly extended his wings and flew away. With the danger gone, Gabriel calmly checked the flock of chickens.

"Good for you, Gabriel!" Kitty shouted. "I'll write about you in my journal. You are the defender of the flock! We're going to need all you chickens to get through the year."

Cleaver barked loudly but did not approach the rooster, for he had also felt his spurs.

Rebecca, not William, appeared with the gun.

"It's all right, Mama. A chicken hawk tried to breakfast on a chick, but Gabriel fought him off," Kitty called, as if it was only a small matter.

Rebecca waved to her and said, "Good," then added, "You will need to feed the animals this morning, Kitty. William isn't feeling well."

Kitty froze. "Fever!" she whispered. "Please God, don't let it be fever. It just can't be."

Blossom Prairie was a beautiful and pleasant land, but it seemed to constantly test the family's courage to remain on it. They had been told that Texas was a raw frontier. And they had expected to face hard work, loneliness, crop failure, and many other hardships. Unknown to them, though, a far more deadly enemy plagued this fertile land. It seemed to ride on the waves and ripples of the Red River, unseen by man. Silently, it would sweep down on the prairie and touch the lives of the hard-work-

35

ing, God-fearing people like an ugly, evil storm. First it would rake the bodies of its victims, causing them to shake with chills. Then it would burn that agonizing body with fever. Some folks called it prairie fever. The Garners had seen it cruelly strike many of their neighbors, and they were concerned that their own family may be stricken.

"Kitty," Rebecca called, "did you hear me?"

"Yes, Mama," she responded. Kitty was still deeply worried as she put her journal down and walked toward the corral. "William doesn't have to have the fever," she whispered, trying to push her fear away. "He could just have a headache."

In the corral, Kitty walked up to Zona and began to rub her on the nose. "Zona," she whispered, "I loved you the moment I saw you. I love you even more because you remind Mama of her horse, Ginger, and give her happy dreams for our future." Kitty affectionately hugged Zona's neck and gave her one last pat on the back, then fed the other horse, the oxen, and Suli.

She could see a light through the cabin window, and thought how warm and inviting it looked. As she slipped inside she saw her mother, cutting biscuits to put into the Dutch oven.

"Kitty, you were up before daybreak. Where have you been?" her mother asked.

"I wanted to see the prairie in the first light of morning, so I could describe it in my journal. Mama," she asked suddenly, "are you glad that we moved to Blossom Prairie?"

Rebecca stopped working for a moment and said, "Yes, Kitty. It has been something of a struggle to get started here, but the prairie has many special qualities." Then she added, "Your journal must have many adventures to relate by now."

"Yes, ma'am," Kitty said, but she pursued her questioning. "Are you worried about how we will make it through the winter, Mama?"

36

"Yes, Kitty," Rebecca answered solemnly. "It does concern me." She hesitated for several moments before speaking again. "Kitty," she said softly, and Kitty could see the sadness in her mother's face. "We may have to sell Zona."

"No, Mama!" Kitty cried, as tears pierced her eyes.

"She is the only thing we have that would bring enough money for supplies and seeds for next year," Rebecca told her.

"Isn't there some other way, Mama?" Kitty asked in a strained voice. "It is so wonderful to have Zona here with us."

"I'll think on it, Kitty," Rebecca responded. "If there is any way we can make it without selling her, of course we'll do it." Rebecca smiled and Kitty felt better.

"We'll think of a way, Mama," Kitty said happily. "I just know that we will." She turned around to greet Mary and Louisa as they came into the kitchen. "Good morning," she called.

"Morning," both girls mumbled sleepily.

"Kitty, you will have time to do the milking before breakfast, and Louisa can gather the eggs," Rebecca instructed her daughters.

Kitty watched Rebecca place the biscuits in the Dutch oven, then put hot coals on top of the lid. "Where is William?" she asked. She had not been able to push the fear of fever from her mind.

"He is not feeling well, and I told him to get a little more sleep this morning," Rebecca replied. She saw the concern on Kitty's face and added, "It's probably just a summer cold."

Kitty's face brightened, and she smiled. "Zona expects a lump of sugar when I go to the corral, Mama. May I have some?" Her spirits had risen with her mother's statement.

Rebecca gave her a fond look and said, "Yes, but not too much, Kitty. I will need some to make a cake for Sunday dinner, and I don't know when we can buy more."

Kitty opened the lid of the sugar barrel and took out a small amount. Then she picked up the milk bucket and started out the cabin door. Louisa followed with the egg basket, and the two girls walked toward the small chicken house.

They could hear the hens cackling contentedly as they followed Gabriel about the yard. "They sound happy now, Louisa, but earlier they were attacked by a chicken hawk," Kitty informed her sister.

"What happened?" Louisa asked with interest.

"Gabriel fought that old hawk and wounded him. Then he sent him flying away from here."

Louisa smiled and looked at Gabriel with greater interest. "I'm glad Gabriel was not drunk," she said, and both girls laughed.

Louisa opened the chicken house door and walked in. Two hens were sitting on eggs, waiting for them to hatch.

Kitty could hear her younger sister talking to the hens as she gathered eggs. She swung her milk bucket about and walked past the chicken house. As she approached the corral, the horses ran up to the rail fence to greet her. Zona arrived first. Each day, Kitty gave her something to eat and rubbed her soft, moist nose. The filly always showed her appreciation.

"Hello again, Zona," Kitty said softly. "I hope we never, *never* have to part with you." She hugged Zona and walked through the corral gate toward the cow. "I can't visit with you now, Zona, for I have work to do."

Suli was still eating some hay in her stall as Kitty drew up the stool and began to milk her. When she finished, she turned Suli out of the corral to graze on the green grass. She patted Zona on the nose again and took the milk pail to the cabin. Then she joined the family at the table.

"This time next year, we'll have lots of eggs on the table for breakfast," Rebecca announced cheerfully.

"Will we be able to buy flour for biscuits, Mama?" Mary asked.

"If we can't afford to buy flour, we'll have cornbread for breakfast," Rebecca responded, as if it did not matter.

"Maybe the little Indian people will come and help us," Charlie said. Kitty noticed that her mother no longer scolded them for talking about the little people.

"We have to invite them first," Louisa reminded him.

"Will we have fried chicken for breakfast too?" John Nance asked.

"We'll have fried chicken too, son," Rebecca said and passed the biscuits to William.

"No, thank you, Mama. I'm not hungry. This cup of coffee is all I want this morning."

Rebecca observed her oldest son closely. "You didn't eat much for supper last night, William, and you need to have something in your stomach."

"I'm all right, Mama. I'm just not hungry," William said as he got up from the table.

Kitty noticed that her brother's face looked pale, and she knew that he was not well. He had been very impatient with her and the other children lately. Fear wedged in her throat. Jim Wilkins had died of the fever last week, and several other people on the prairie had taken to their beds with it.

Rebecca did not take her eyes off William, and Kitty could see the worried expression on her face. She knew her mother shared her fear about the fever.

"Take the day off and rest, William," Rebecca said. "There is a lot of sickness in Red River County right now. Cousin Tom just came down with the chills and fever and is flat of his back. I don't want you to get sick, William. You had best go and lie down for a while."

Suddenly, William fell on the table. Before anyone could move, his limp body slipped to the floor. Panic-stricken, all of the children jumped up.

"William," Rebecca called, as she leaned over him and rubbed his face. William did not respond and Re-

39

becca quickly turned to the other children. "Help me carry him to his bed," she commanded.

Kitty, Mary, and Louisa helped their mother carry William's limp body. John Nance and Charlie followed, and tears streamed down their faces.

"What's wrong with William?" Charlie asked.

"I think he has the fever, son," Rebecca answered in a strange, weak voice.

The words had been spoken. Fear gripped Kitty as she stood beside her brother's bed. They all sighed with relief when he opened his eyes and began to stir about.

"I feel real cold, Mama," he said.

"Mary," Rebecca called gently, "get another quilt for your brother."

She felt of William's forehead, then slowly walked away from his bed. Kitty followed her into the kitchen and watched her open the medicine chest. Rebecca's face did not mask her worry as she closed the chest and turned around. She held a small bottle in her hand.

"Kitty," she said in a low voice, "we only have enough chill cure for one dose. I gave most of what we had to Betsy when Cousin Tom came down with the fever. Nearly every family on the prairie has at least one member in bed with fever sickness. It would be useless to try to borrow chill cure from our neighbors."

"What will we do, Mama?" Kitty asked in a whisper.

"I'll make some sassafras tea and give it to William when he has taken the final dose of chill cure. Then . . . then . . ." Suddenly, she turned to Kitty and said, "Kitty, you and Mary must ride to Clarksville to buy some chill cure. It will take a day to get there and purchase it. You can spend the night with Mrs. Jones and start home tomorrow morning. Start saddling the horses, while I pack a lunch for you," she said. "I'll send Mary out to help." Then she put her hand on Kitty's shoulder. "I don't want to send you girls out alone, but there is no one else I can send, Kitty."

Kitty and Mary quickly saddled the horses, then

rode them to the cabin door. Rebecca handed them some biscuits and bacon wrapped in a cotton cloth. She also gave Kitty some money tied up in a handkerchief. She stood by Zona for a moment and stroked her long, silky mane.

"She is truly beautiful," Rebecca said thoughtfully. Suddenly, she turned to both girls and said, "Be very careful, girls."

"We will, Mama." Kitty felt that there was something her mother meant to say but didn't.

"The druggist may try to sell you lungwort or wild cherry bark. But don't you buy it," Rebecca instructed Kitty. "Only the chill cure medicine, quinine, will help this fever."

"Yes, Mama," Kitty said.

"Stop when the sun is overhead and have lunch. Be sure to stop and rest on the way, and return as quickly as possible."

"Don't worry, Mama. We'll get the chill cure and be back before you know it," the girls assured her.

41

5.

The Chill Cure

Kitty and Mary rode their horses at a gallop onto the trail that would lead them to Clarksville, the county seat of Red River County. Zona wanted to go faster, but Kitty gently pulled on her reins and kept her in pace with the other horse.

A few prairie flowers were still blooming, and sweet, pungent smells surrounded them on all sides along the trail. The woods jutted out like islands on the prairie, and the girls would sometimes ride beneath the shade of the large bois d'arc, pecan, or oak trees. They saw rabbits and other small animals scurry for cover as they rode along.

After riding in silence for a while, Kitty knew that Mary was as worried as she was about William.

"William will get well, Mary," Kitty tried to assure her sister. "As soon as we return with the chill cure, he will begin to get better right away. That medicine helps people get over the fever. By tomorrow night, we'll be back home and you can see for yourself."

"I sure hope you're right, Kitty."

"We are doing all that we can to help him," Kitty

said and made herself smile. "Look, Mary, there's a stream up ahead. We can water the horses and have our lunch." They stopped by a small creek and ate the lunch Rebecca had prepared for them.

It was late afternoon when they rode into Clarksville. The entire family had been there to buy supplies shortly after they arrived on Blossom Prairie. The girls had not been into town since. It was a treat to see the sights, but Kitty and Mary lost little time looking about. They rode past the frame houses and the old stone courthouse, then reined their horses near the mercantile store. There they dismounted and tied the horses to the hitching post.

Two men, walking toward them on the board sidewalk, tipped their hats and walked on. A lady, carrying a basket of goods, walked out of the mercantile store. She smiled at the girls and went on her way. They smiled back, then walked down the street to Judson's Drug Store. A wide sign over the counter read: "Judson's Chemical Extracts." Bottles and tins of medicines filled the store. There were also some dried leaves hanging in one corner of the store.

Kitty and Mary looked about in wonderment. All of the odors and the medicines seemed strange to them. The *Standard Newspaper,* selling for ten cents, lay on the counter. Kitty read it while they waited for the druggist to help an elderly woman at the counter. The Democratic Party was running Franklin Pierce for president, while the Whigs supported Winfield Scott. There was also a writeup about Governor Bell of Texas. The capital in Austin seemed a long way off, and Kitty did not know much about politics. She picked up copies of *The Great British Quarterlies* and *The Backwood's Magazine* that were for sale. They had articles of subjects far away, and there was some mention of King George IV.

"Good day to you young ladies," the druggist greeted them. "What can I do for you today?"

Kitty stepped up to the counter and spoke without

hesitation. "My brother has the fever and we need some chill cure. We live on Blossom Prairie and have ridden all day to purchase it."

"That so?" the druggist remarked, then scratched his chin and frowned. "Been lots of folks down with the fever. Nearly always that way after a big rain. Fact is, there's been so much fever that I sold out of that medicine last week. I sent to Jefferson to get more, but it'll be two, maybe even three weeks before I get a new supply from Jefferson. I'm mighty sorry about that, but that's the way things are. Now, to my way of thinking, wild cherry bark will do just as good as chill cure." He picked up a bottle of red-colored liquid and pointed to the label. "You can see right here that this medicine claims to cure coughs, spitting of blood, night sweats, asthma, and liver complaints." The girls watched with interest as he took the top from the bottle and took a drink. "Tastes good too," he said, and grinned at them.

"Mama told us to buy the chill cure medicine, quinine," Kitty informed him, and added, "Nothing else."

"I am sorry, but I don't have any chill cure."

The girls exchanged looks. Kitty swallowed hard and turned to the druggist. He shrugged his shoulders and gave them a sympathetic look.

"Is there anyone in town who may have some chill cure?" Kitty asked hopefully.

"Not a soul," he responded sadly. "I have checked everywhere in town. Not a single merchant here has any. We're all waiting for the chill cure to come with our other supplies. We're expecting our goods to be brought in by wagons from Jefferson. The supplier there gets chill cure from New Orleans by steamboat. That's the best I can do," he concluded.

"But . . . but," Kitty started.

The druggist shook his head and said, "I sure am sorry about your brother."

Kitty nodded, and the girls left the store with downcast faces.

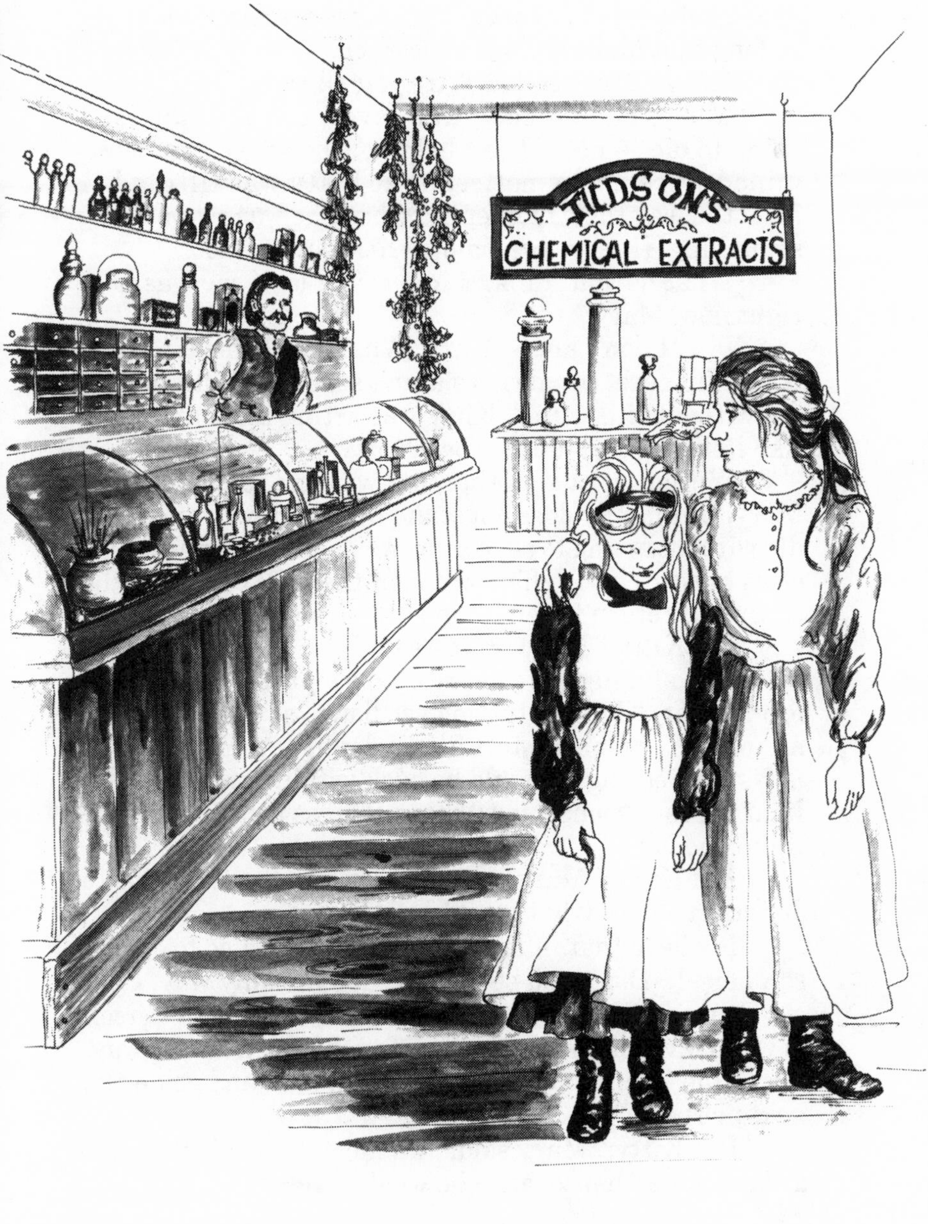
JUDSON'S
CHEMICAL EXTRACTS

"Kitty," Mary asked, "what are we going to do?"

Kitty did not answer, but she had a far-off look in her eyes as she calmly stroked Zona's mane. She stood there so long that Mary became concerned.

"Kitty," Mary called. "Are you all right?"

"Mary, Papa died with a fever, but William isn't going to die — not if I can help it," she spoke in a determined voice. Mary noticed that Kitty was tilting her head the way their mother did when she was set on doing something. Her eyes resembled her mother's too.

"What do you think Mama would do if she was here right now, Mary?"

"I . . . I don't know, Kitty. What could she do? There is no chill cure. Besides, we aren't sure that William will die without chill cure." Kitty was acting more and more like Rebecca, and it disturbed Mary.

"William is our brother and we can't take a chance, Mary. Our family does not stand by and allow someone to die without acting to save him. We do what we must. One of us must ride to Jefferson to get the chill cure, and the other will return to tell Mama," she announced.

"No, Kitty," Mary protested.

As if she had not heard Mary's protest, Kitty informed her, "Zona is the fastest horse, so I must go. I'll allow her to rest and start before daylight tomorrow. She is fast and strong. I should be back within four days. William needs it sooner, but that will be as fast as I can get there and back."

"But Kitty," Mary protested again, "you can't ride to Jefferson alone. What would Mama say?"

"I believe that in my place Mama would go to Jefferson herself. Don't you see, Mary? It's the only way. Cousin Tom said that the trail from Clarksville to Jefferson is well traveled and there are a few farms along the way. I can stop, spend the night at one of them, and go on the next morning."

"But Kitty," Mary said, "we have to spend the night at Mrs. Jones' house, and she won't allow it."

"She doesn't have to know. My mind is made up, Mary. Tomorrow you can ride back to Blossom Prairie and tell Mama what I've done."

The next morning, a good two hours before daylight, Kitty slipped out of bed, picked up a small candle, and saddled Zona. She led her out of town until she reached the trail, then climbed into the saddle. Holding the reins loosely, she gave Zona her head.

Kitty leaned forward and whispered into Zona's ear. "We're going to Jefferson, Zona, and it's up to you to get us there in a hurry. William has the fever and we must get the medicine that will make him well."

She moved gracefully with the horse's rhythm as they rode swiftly along the trail. Long, auburn hair blew freely about her face, and the long skirt of her cotton dress whipped about her legs. Her face was flushed with excitement, and her eyes were firmly set on the horizon. As she leaned forward on the horse, she urged her to run even faster. She knew how Rebecca must have felt when she rode Ginger.

A bird soared overhead and Kitty felt as if she were flying with it. "I'll race you," she called to the bird. By the time sunlight streaked through the trees, she was too far away for Mrs. Jones to send a rider after her. The trail was well traveled, but Kitty seemed to be the only rider on it. After they had ridden awhile, she pulled on Zona's reins and slowed her down. "Save your strength, Zona. Jefferson is seventy miles away. We have a long way to go."

Kitty had never been on the trail before, but she had heard about it. The people on Blossom Prairie hauled their cotton in ox-drawn wagons to Jefferson and sold it to buyers who came in on the steamboats. It took a long time to travel to Jefferson by wagon, but Kitty knew that Zona could cover the distance much quicker. Even the stagecoach could make twenty miles a day, so she knew Zona could do better.

Kitty saw chimney smoke from a farm house but did

47

not stop. When the sun was overhead, she stopped by a little stream and rested. Berry vines grew along the creek bank, and she picked some to eat. Zona grazed on the tender grass, and they both drank from the creek. Then they approached the trail again.

Soon Kitty saw several riders coming toward her. She had heard stories about mean men and Indians on the trail. She knew that they had not seen her, so she pulled Zona off into a wooded area and waited for them to pass. They were a coarse, dirty-looking lot, and each of them drank from a bottle. Kitty waited until they disappeared from sight before she emerged from the woods and continued her journey.

Finally, Kitty crossed the Sulphur River. When she was on the south bank, she stopped and looked back across the river. Loneliness crept over her as she looked northwest toward Blossom Prairie. She had felt very brave when she started out, but now she was thinking of the stories she had heard about renegade Indians and highwaymen preying on travelers. She wished for someone to talk to and ride beside her as she rode into Titus County.

Zona moved along at a steady pace. Kitty soon tired of watching the birds fly about and seeing small animals dart across the road. The sun beat down on her and the heat made her uncomfortable. From time to time she would doze off, only to wake quickly at a slight jolt.

The day moved on to midafternoon and she did not see another farm. She began to believe that she may have to sleep on the trail alone. She had never been away from her family at night before. A feeling of fear and loneliness set upon her.

6.

Meeting Big Foot Wallace

As she rode downhill, she spotted a horse on the trail. Mental images of Indians and highwaymen caused her to hesitate and study the scene before her. The horse was saddled for riding, but there was no rider. She looked about carefully, but no one was in sight. A canvas bag hung from the saddle horn, making a jangling noise, and a rawhide structure resembling a deer leg hung beside it. She approached the animal cautiously.

"Whoa, boy," she called and reached down to pick up his reins. "Where is your master?" she asked.

The horse pulled about on the reins, and Kitty felt that he wanted her to follow him. She turned him loose and followed him into a clump of trees. There she saw the outline of a large man on the ground. A saddlebag lay beside him, and its contents had been scattered about.

"Hello, there!" she called to him.

The man did not answer. Kitty waited for a few minutes, wondering if she shouldn't ride away. He may be one of the highwaymen she had heard her neighbors speak of. On the other hand, she thought, he may be sick and unable to answer. The horse nudged the body on the ground, and Kitty rode up to him.

"Hello!" she called again, but there was no response. She saw blood running down his forehead, and the sleeve of his shirt was drenched in blood.

"Mister," Kitty called, "can you hear me?" He did not answer, so Kitty slowly got down from her horse. Cautiously, she leaned over him and observed him closely. There was a large, bloody gash on his forehead, and she suspected he had been shot in the arm. Blood colored the ground next to him. She could see his head move slightly, and knew that he was still alive.

"You're hurt real bad, Mister, but I'll do what I can for you," Kitty whispered. She took a cotton cloth from her pocket and dipped it in a nearby stream. Then she washed the man's face and cleaned the dried blood from an open wound on his forehead. When she moved his arm, he began to groan. Then his hand formed into a fist. Kitty jumped up and quickly moved away from him. Not knowing what he intended to do, she watched with concern as he opened his eyes.

He gave her a startled look, and his face began to soften. "Why, you're jest a little girl!"

"My name's Kitty Garner," she said, relieved that he didn't plan to hit her.

"Wallace," he said between clenched teeth. "William Alexander Anderson Wallace. Some folks call me Big Foot Wallace."

"Big Foot Wallace!" Kitty said in amazement and looked down at his feet for confirmation. "Why, you're a Texas hero. Lots of folks know about you. You were a Ranger captain, a scout, and an Indian fighter."

"Yep, some say so," he declared and grabbed his arm as pain covered his face.

"You're hurt real bad, Big Foot — I mean Mr. Wallace," Kitty told him.

"I can't rightly say what part 'o me hurts the most, my head or my arm." He looked at Kitty as if he had just

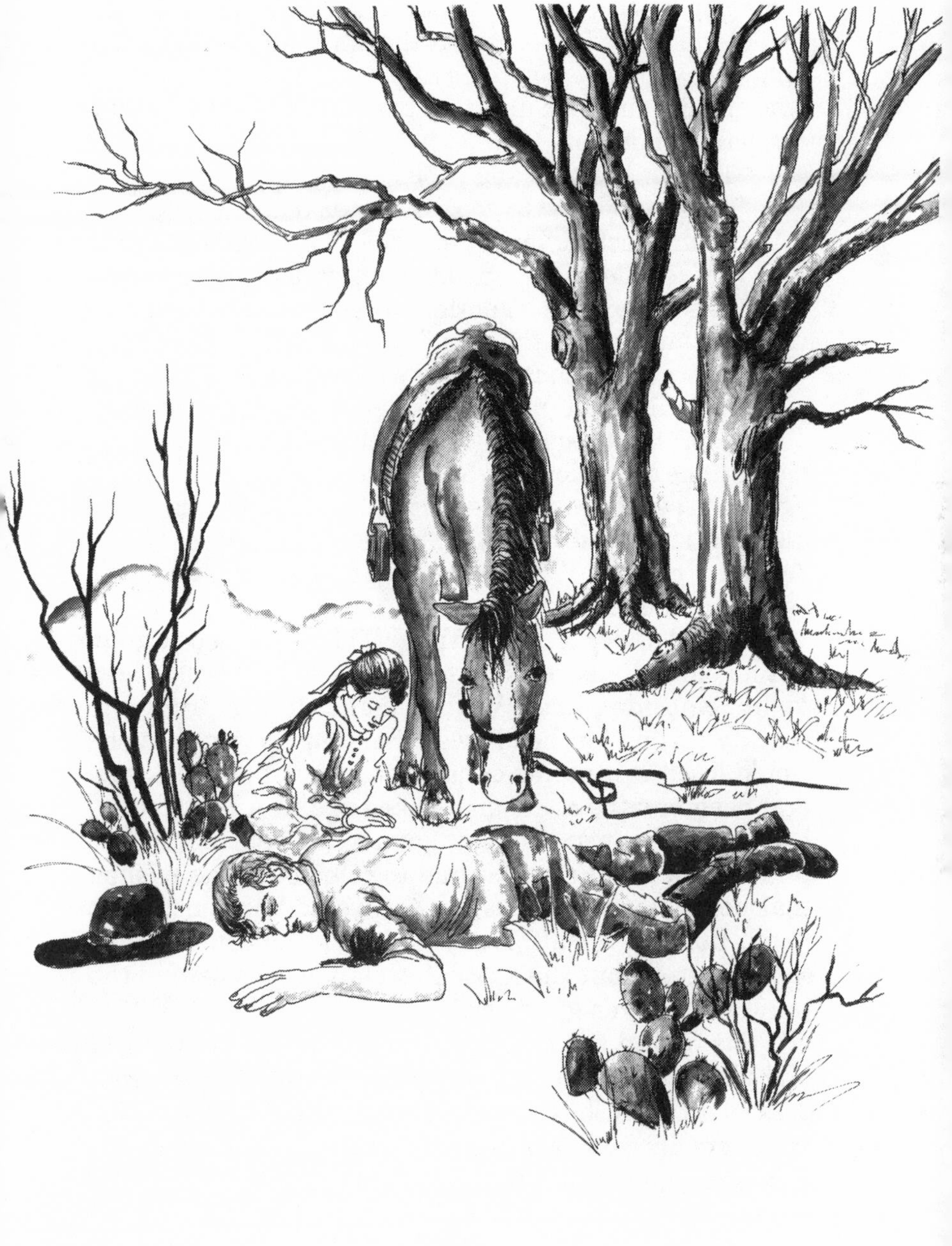

seen her. Then he began to pull himself up into a sitting position, with his back against a tree. "I'm gonna need some help, girl. Where are your folks?"

"I am traveling alone on the trail, Mr. Wallace. I'm on my way to Jefferson," she said. "The last farm I passed was about five or six miles up the trail. I'm not sure how far Jefferson is from here."

"Too far," he said and rubbed his arm.

"What happened to you?" Kitty asked.

"Bushwhacked," he responded. "Bushwhacked by a bunch of low-down — " Suddenly aware of Kitty's presence, he explained in a gentler voice, "I was knocked over the head and shot in the arm."

Kitty noticed that his face was getting very pale. "Is — is the bullet still in your arm?" she asked.

"Yep," he responded, "and it's been in there too long. Gotta come out. I don't rightly know how I'm gonna manage," he said and appraised Kitty, as if he was trying to decide if she could help him. Suddenly he added, "But I reckon I gotta." When he had finished speaking, he slipped to the ground and did not move.

"Mr. Wallace . . . Mr. Wallace!" Kitty called to him, but he did not answer. She tore his sleeve off and looked at his wounded arm. With a sickening feeling, she quickly turned her head away. She felt certain that she would lose the contents of her stomach, but she took several deep breaths of air and looked again. A large bullet hole was in his arm, and an ugly red area surrounded it. She knew that the bullet had to come out. She wished that her mother was here, for she would know just what to do. But she wasn't. Kitty had little experience with these matters, but she knew this man needed help in the worst way. It was up to her.

She built a fire and began to pick up the contents of Mr. Wallace's saddlebag. She didn't know what the robbers had taken, but they left many items behind. Her eyes were drawn to a book that was partly inside the saddlebag. Curious, Kitty took a look at the title. "Why!" she whispered, "It's *Oliver Twist*." She took a quick look at the big man lying on the ground and wondered why he had this book.

As she picked up the saddlebag, a bottle fell from it. She quickly read the label. "It's chill cure! Oh!" she said out loud. "Mr. Wallace, as soon as you are awake, I'll ask to buy some of this for William. I may not have to go to Jefferson after all." She picked up a sturdy knife and placed it next to the fire. Then she took the canvas and rawhide bags from the horse. The latter contained water, which she would need in order to wash up.

Kitty passed the knife blade over the flames of the fire several times. Trying to bolster her courage, she breathed deeply and began probing the wounded area with the point of the knife. She hated sticking the knife into him, and wished desperately that she didn't have to. There was no laudanum to make him sleep, but mercifully, Mr. Wallace was unconscious. She soon felt the knife touch the bullet, and she began to pry it out.

Perspiration popped out on Kitty's forehead, and she still felt nauseated. She was very tired, and she prayed for strength to finish her gruesome task. The bullet had gone quite deep, and it took several minutes to pry it to the surface of his arm. When it was out, she put the knife into the flame again until it was very hot. Then she pressed the blade into the wound again, as she had seen her mother do. "That will stop the bleeding," she said aloud, as if to assure herself.

Kitty cleaned his arm the best she could and put a cotton cloth around the wound. Wallace remained unconscious throughout the procedure. She banked up the fire — and waited. Very tired, she soon fell asleep on the ground. She was awakened when the man began to stir about.

"You still here, girl?" he asked.

"Yes, sir," Kitty responded. "How do you feel, sir?"

"Like I been tied between two wild hosses and pulled apart. I musta passed out. One thing is for shore, I'm gonna have to cut this here bullet outta my arm," he said, and started to get up.

"The bullet has been removed, Mr. Wallace," Kitty reported. He gave her a puzzled look, and she explained. "I took it out."

"What's that you're sayin'?" he asked, looking at his bandaged arm. Confused, he looked at Kitty again. "Why, a little slip of a girl like you . . . what would you know about cuttin' a bullet outta a feller?"

"I helped my mother remove a bullet from my brother William's arm. His wound was similar to yours," she explained and added, "and he got well."

Big Foot Wallace began to laugh. "He did, did he?"

"Yes, sir."

"Well, I'm mighty glad to hear that news," he said and grinned. He watched her with greater interest and abruptly asked, "What ya doin' out here on the trail by yourself, girl?"

"My brother William has the prairie fever, and I was on my way to Jefferson to purchase some chill cure."

"Where do you live?" he asked.

"Blossom Prairie in Red River County," Kitty answered. "There has been so much fever sickness in our area that the medicine has all been used up. The stores in Clarksville didn't have any more. No one else did, either," she added.

"So ya jest tore out and headed fer Jefferson," he said, as if he were talking to himself. He watched her for a full minute. She was a curiosity for sure. But she wasn't flighty. She stuck by him and brought him around. Then she took the bullet out and patched him up, the best she could. "You got spunk, girl, I'll say that fer ya. I'm much obliged to you for fixin' my arm. Looks like ya did a purty good job too."

"You're welcome, Mr. Wallace," Kitty responded, then abruptly stated, "I'd like to buy some of the chill cure from you, Mr. Wallace."

"Chill cure?" he asked.

"Yes, sir. You have a bottle of chill cure in your saddlebag." He looked at her sternly, and she quickly explained. "Oh, I didn't look through your things deliberately. I saw the chill cure while I was looking for your knife. It would save me a trip to Jefferson," she said.

His face softened. "Why, girl, you can have that medicine. The storekeeper outfittin' me in Austin sold it ta me. Said I might need it afore I got back that way."

"Thank you, sir," Kitty said.

"Don't mention it."

"Did the men rob you of anything valuable?" Kitty asked.

"Rob me?" He seemed startled, as if he had not considered the possibility. Then he looked at his feet, and a sly smile crossed his face. "Nope, they didn't find what they was a lookin' fer. Nope, they shore couldn't find it," he said and chuckled to himself.

Big Foot Wallace's face twisted in pain, and Kitty looked at him with concern.

"Ya had a long ride today. With fixin' me up and all, I reckon you're plumb wore out, girl."

"I'm all right," Kitty said. "Are you in pain?"

"Yep, hurts a bit. But I reckon I'll make it."

"Would you like to read the book to help forget the pain?" Kitty asked.

"Book?" he asked.

"I found *Oliver Twist* in your saddlebag."

A strange expression of awareness crossed Mr. Wallace's face, causing Kitty to sit up straight.

"What did ya say your name was?" he asked sharply.

"Kitty Garner."

"What's your ma's name?"

"Rebecca Garner."

"Well, I'll be dogged!" he declared, and began to laugh. Kitty wondered if he was out of his head.

"That book in my saddlebag belongs to your folks, Kitty. I . . . I've got ta use it fer a while. Then I am to take it to a Garner family on Blossom Prairie. I swear, but life shore has a way 'o puttin' things together. Yep, it shore does."

In a moment of insight, Kitty understood and blurted out, "Senator Sam Houston borrowed my *Oliver Twist* book a few months back. He said he would send another one to replace it. Mr. Wallace, you must have been sent by Sam Houston."

"Yep," he said and looked on all sides of him. "It's a fact, Kitty, but I don't want it known. I can tell ya one thing — I'll be traveling in your direction."

"That will be just grand, Mr. Wallace. I'll be glad of your company. As soon as you have rested we can ride on."

He did not speak as they rode, and Kitty suspected that he was in pain. He dozed off once and she was very concerned about him. She knew that he had lost a lot of blood and was weak, though he would not admit it. She was afraid that he would fall off his horse, so she began to sing to keep him awake.

"What ya hollerin' about?" he asked gruffly.

"I'm singing to keep you awake," she responded honestly.

"I'd be obliged if ya wouldn't do that right now. I reckon talking would be tolerable, though. Tell me about your folks. Sam Houston spoke highly of yore ma, Rebecca, and her kin."

"My mother is a very fine lady, Mr. Wallace. She was a Walpole and she knew General Andrew Jackson in Tennessee," Kitty said proudly. "Papa died five years ago while we were living near Nashville, Tennessee, and we had a hard time on the farm there. Mama knew that she would have to sell off the farm land just to get by. She wanted her children to have land to prosper on, and she had a dream about a farm on Blossom Prairie. All of us talked it over and decided to make the long trip to Texas. We got our farm started, but we lost our cotton crop due to floods."

"How'd you get to Texas?" he asked.

"Mama bought a new spring wagon and two young oxen, making four in all. We joined a wagon train at Nashville and traveled by way of the Natchez Trace for a piece, then crossed the Mississippi River at Helena, Arkansas. We traveled south until we crossed the Red River at Fulton, Arkansas."

"Some of yore mama's kinfolks come with ya, did they?" he asked.

"No, sir, just Mama and us six children."

He gave her a surprised look, and declared, "I'll be danged! That's quite a trip fer a woman and a buncha kids ta make. Yore ma must be a mighty strong woman."

"Yes, sir," Kitty said, "we made it just fine."

Mr. Wallace let out a low whistle that amused Kitty, but he had asked about her family and she wanted to know about him. "Would you tell me some of the things you have done, Mr. Wallace?" she asked.

"Well, now, first one thing then t'nother. I got ta Texas jest about the time the Texas Revolution had ended, so I didn't take part in that fight. My brother was killed in it, though. I been a Texas Ranger, a carpenter, and a soldier. I done some scoutin', and Injun fightin' too. I was a stagecoach driver on a run between San Antone and El Paso when I got a message to meet ole Sam Houston close to Austin for a parley."

"Why are you on the trail, Mr. Wallace?" she asked.

"I got some business to do fer ole Sam, and it's business I don't care to talk about," he said gruffly and took a big chew of tobacco.

"I'd sure like to know about the black and white beans," Kitty told him.

"Well, it was back a ways when Texas was still a republic. We was a havin' a heap 'o trouble along our southwestern border with the Mexicans, Injuns, and outlaws. President Lamar got ole Jack Hays to raise a company of Rangers to protect that border. I was one of the first Rangers to join up. I had me a horse worth one hundred

57

dollars. I could shoot and ride good, so Hays took me on. We headquartered in San Antone.

"In 1842 some Mexican troops invaded Texas and captured San Antone. Well, Hays and about two hundred of us reclaimed the city, and sent them Mexicans hightailin' it across the Rio Grande. I was a part 'o the 1843 expedition that marched to Mexico to show them that we didn't take kindly ta them invadin' Texas. We was supposed ta turn back, but about three hundred of us kept a going. It was called the Mier expedition. We captured the village of Mier and whopped a few 'o them Mexicans. But we were surprised by a large force of 'em. They captured us, put irons on us, and started marching us toward Mexico City. I managed to escape with some others, but them Mexicans caught us agin. Santa Anna ordered that every tenth man of us was ta be shot. They brought out a jar filled with beans. They told us if we drew a black bean, we'd be shot, but if we got a white bean, we'd live. I reckon you can see I drew a white bean," he concluded.

Kitty listened with fascination. She could see that he was weary, and she did not press him to tell her more.

Soon they stopped by a stream. The horses needed to rest and graze some before going on. It was getting late, and Kitty was anxious to be on the road back to her family with the chill cure. She knew that it would not be safe to ride at night, so she began to look for a farm where they could stop for the night.

7.

Molasses

They crossed the Sulfur River and headed northwest into Red River County. Kitty felt better, for she was that much closer to delivering the chill cure to William. When she saw smoke twirling in the air over the trees, she knew it had to be coming from a chimney. She guided Zona off the trail.

"There is smoke coming from a house up ahead, Mr. Wallace. Perhaps the people living there will be able to tend your arm and put us up for the night."

"Do you know these people, Kitty?" he asked suspiciously. He seemed more alert than he had been.

"No, but most Texans are friendly and will invite traveling strangers to spend the night. They may invite us to eat supper too," she said. She was very hungry.

Kitty pulled the reins of her horse, and Mr. Wallace followed her off the trail. She noticed that he looked pale and was slouched over in the saddle. She soon spotted a small cabin nestled among some shade trees and beside a well-tended field of cotton. Kitty rode in that direction and approached the cabin slowly.

59

No one was in the field, nor moving about the cabin, but she brought Zona to a halt and called out, "Hello! Is there anyone home?" Although no one answered, she felt that someone was inside the cabin. She thought she heard movement from inside.

Kitty sat in the saddle several minutes and waited. Big Foot Wallace rested his hand on his gun and looked about anxiously. Tired, hungry and discouraged, Kitty began to turn Zona about to ride away. Suddenly, she heard a voice from the cabin.

"Whar ya goin'?"

Wallace sat very still and focused his attention on the cabin door. Kitty turned about to see a very large woman with a pleasant smile emerge from the cabin. She was dressed in red calico.

"Why, you folks look friendly enough," she said and laughed, "and all the time I was a cowering in that cabin scared outta my wits."

Kitty sat still as the woman approached them and began to observe Zona with interest. "Pardon my manners," she said, "but I don't often see the likes of such a fine hoss. My name's Amanda Thompson, and I'd be mighty happy to have yore company. Get offa them hosses."

"I'm Kitty Garner, and this is Mr. Wallace," Kitty replied with relief as she got down from the saddle. "We would be grateful if you would allow us to spend the night here."

"Shore, child," Amanda called out in a gruff but friendly voice. She turned her attention to Big Foot Wallace. "Mister, ya look like ya been walloped good and sound. Step down from yore hoss and come on in." To Kitty, she said, "Young lady, there's fresh hay in that there lean-to if you want to tend to yore hosses. While you're a doing that, I'll fix us a bite to eat. I wasn't hungry before. But with company to set table with me, I guess my appetite has jest perked up."

Kitty rubbed the horses down and put hay out for

them. As she returned to the cabin, she saw Big Foot Wallace spread a blanket under a tree and lie down. She joined Amanda in the cabin, where the large woman was pouring cornbread batter into a Dutch oven.

"Find a stool and set yoreself down, child." Amanda spoke without turning away from the fireplace. "That big feller didn't want to eat none. He jest wanted to sleep. He's been shot, ain't he?" she asked abruptly.

Kitty nodded.

"I reckon he needs rest then. Most likely, he'll feel better by morning," she said. "Got some good venison stew in the other pot. I'll heat it up, and it'll taste good with the cornbread."

Kitty sat down at the table and looked about the cabin. It was very similar to her home. There was a spinning wheel in one corner of the room and braided rugs on the floor. Ropes hanging from rafters in the ceiling supported some quilting frames.

"Won't take but about ten minutes for that cornbread to cook, then we'll eat. Got a good batch of homemade corn syrup too," she said proudly. "I made it myself from our own corn stalks."

"Do you live alone?" Kitty asked.

"My husband, Eli, went to Jefferson to trade for another ox and a good milk cow. Been gone four days now, and I'm gettin' a mite worried about him," she said and turned her attention to Kitty. "You say your name's Kitty Garner?"

"Yes," Kitty replied.

"I ain't never heard of a Garner family living here abouts."

"I'm from Blossom Prairie," Kitty explained. "I met Mr. Wallace on the trail last evening. He was injured badly. Since he was on his way to Blossom Prairie, he decided to ride with me."

"Well, now," Amanda asked, "what was a young one like you doing on the trail all by yoreself in the first place?"

61

"My brother William is down with the fever, and we didn't have any chill cure at home. Mama sent my sister and me to Clarksville to purchase some, but there was none to be had. The druggist said Jefferson would have some, so I decided to ride to Jefferson to buy it. I . . . I didn't want William to die."

"Why, of course ya don't. But child, Jefferson is a far piece from yore home. Many a mean thing could befall a young one traveling that trail. There's Injuns roamin' about and bad men up to no good. Aside from them with two feet to walk on, there's a whole passel of others — wolves, bear, and worst of all, panthers to prey on a body."

Kitty listened with wide eyes and a measure of concern.

"I know what I'm a sayin'. The first night Eli was gone, a panther come right up ta my door. I knowed he was there 'cause I heard him screamin' like a wild woman. Even in this cabin I was jest as scared as if I'd a been eyeball to eyeball with him. I'm telling you, it ain't right for a young girl to ride on the trail alone. I'm sure that yore mama don't know about it neither," she scolded, while giving Kitty an indignant look.

"No, ma'am, she doesn't know," Kitty said as she cast her eyes toward the table. "Mr. Wallace gave me some chill cure, and I don't have to go to Jefferson," she added.

"I reckon it ain't any of my business," Amanda said in a kinder voice, and got up to serve the dinner.

"The food is very good," Kitty offered after she had eaten some. "I am grateful to you for inviting me to share the meal with you."

"It's my pleasure, girl. I wish Mr. Wallace had felt like eatin'. I like to see a body go to bed with a full belly," Amanda said, her good humor returning. "It gets real lonesome around here, especially with Eli gone. I'd be grateful fer a flock 'o chickens and a rooster to crow and keep me company. We ain't got many neighbors, but this is good farm land. Eli and me, we stayed and turned this old land into a fine farm. We been here three years now and we've had three good cotton harvests. Eli hauls the cotton to Jefferson to sell. Harvest time is my favorite time of the year. That's when we see others that travel this trail on their way to sell cotton in Jefferson. Rest of the time, it's jest plain lonesome."

"Don't you have any children?" Kitty asked.

"There's only Molasses," Amanda said.

"Molasses?"

"He ain't here right now, but you'll meet him. Yep, come dark and he'll be here." She laughed and gave Kitty a sly look.

Kitty watched her with interest and wondered who Molasses was.

"The sun's nearly down, girl, and I reckon ya must be tired. I'm gonna put a candle in the winder fer Eli, case he comes in tonight. Then I'll fix up a pallet fer ya to sleep on."

"Thank you," Kitty said. "I am tired and we must get an early start tomorrow."

As soon as the cabin was quiet, Kitty began to worry about William. She wanted so much for him to get well, and she missed her family terribly. She also felt some remorse because she had not returned to Blossom Prairie as her mother expected. But she was very tired and soon fell asleep.

She didn't know how long she had slept before she heard a low hissing noise at her back. By candlelight she saw the dark shadow of a large creature loom over her pallet. Her first thought was of the little Indian people. But they would not hiss, she decided, and they were in the Indian Territory.

She was afraid to turn around and face the intruder. Instead, she continued to watch the shadow cast by the candlelight and listen to the terrifying hissing noise. Her mind was still fresh with the talk of panthers and bears. With each second the shadow seemed to be growing big-

63

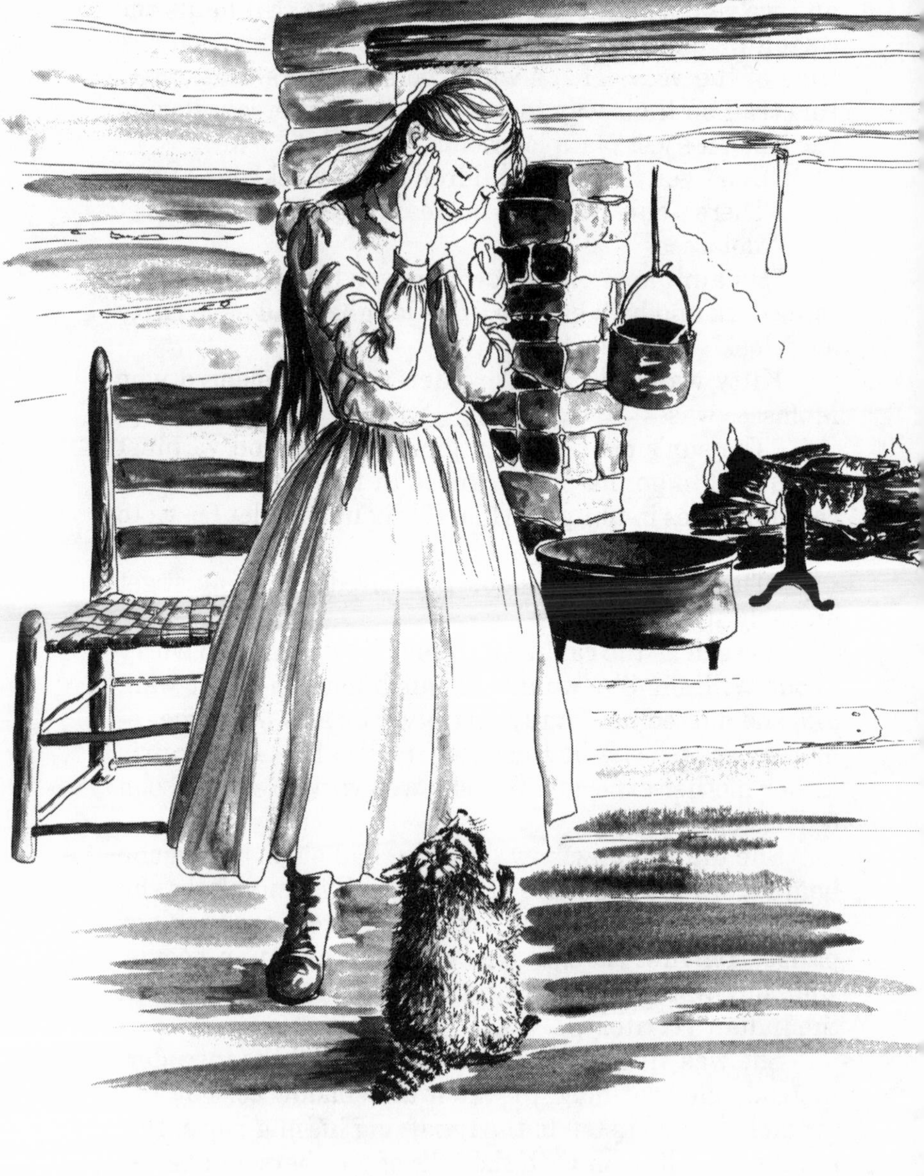

ger, and fear tingled along Kitty's spine and swelled in her throat, choking her. Suddenly, the creature grabbed her by the hair and Kitty found her voice. She screamed as loud as she could.

Amanda was on her feet instantly, scolding Kitty's assailant. "Molasses," she called sternly, "ya let go 'o her. I say turn loose!"

Immediately, the creature released Kitty's hair. She jumped up and moved away from the pallet. Her fear began to lessen as she looked at him. He stood on his hind feet and showed his teeth, but he did not move toward her. There was a small red cap perched on his head. He had a black mask about his eyes, and his forepaws looked like slender human hands.

"Why — why," Kitty said in amazement, "he's a raccoon! He looked so big — that is, his shadow did."

It was then that the door burst open and Big Foot Wallace appeared in the doorway with his pistol drawn. "What's wrong?" he asked.

Amanda laughed. "Ole Molasses, he's harmless. But he ain't used to seein' a stranger sleeping in his house. See, I'll show you," she said, and called to him. "Come here, Molasses." With that, the raccoon jumped into Amanda's arms and hugged her just like a child would.

"Hello, Molasses," Kitty said to him. "I'm Kitty Garner, and I'm your guest for the night. I won't be afraid of you anymore," she added.

"I don't reckon I ever seen a coon do that before," Wallace said, putting his pistol away.

"Molasses knows lots of tricks," Amanda assured them. "He will chase a stick and bring it back to ya too."

"That's mighty fine, ma'am," the big man said. "I reckon I'll turn in."

The next morning Kitty went to a small creek near the cabin to wash up before breakfast. When she returned to the cabin, she knew that someone had come. A horse and an ox were outside, and she heard hens cackling inside. Big Foot Wallace was nowhere in sight and

Kitty was concerned. She walked into the cabin cautiously, wondering if he had decided to leave without her.

"This is my husband, Eli," Amanda said as Kitty entered the room.

The man got up with a wide, friendly smile on his face and extended his hand to Kitty. "Mighty pleased to have you visit with us, Kitty," he said.

"Where is Mr. Wallace?" Amanda asked.

Suddenly, Big Foot Wallace appeared at the cabin door.

"Come in, Mr. Wallace. This is my husband, Eli. He kinda snook up on us."

"Why, I do declare," Eli said, offering his hand to Mr. Wallace. "Big Foot Wallace! It's him Amanda, it's Big Foot Wallace in the flesh!"

"Big Foot Wallace! Why, I knew the name, but I ain't never met the man. I jest didn't know it was you," Amanda declared.

"I'm obliged to your wife for lettin' us rest here fer the night," Wallace said.

"Shore thing," Eli Thompson replied. "You look like ya been winged in the arm and hit over the head."

"I was bushwhacked and left to die, but this little girl here come along and fixed me up."

"That a fact?" Eli looked at Kitty with interest. "Ya'll jest get set ta eat. Amanda is about to fix up some breakfast."

The hens were in a cage near the window, and Kitty walked toward them. "Amanda," she called, "you have some chickens."

"Eli got them in Jefferson," she responded and turned to Mr. Wallace. "You'd best let me change the bandage on that arm 'o yours, Mr. Wallace."

"That's mighty kind of ya," he said, and sat down on a stool while she removed the bandage Kitty had put on it.

"Seems ta be festerin'," Amanda told him. "Looks like the poison's kinda spreading around too. I reckon you're feeling it some, ain't ya?"

"Yep," he replied.

"Ya might do well to stay here fer a spell till ya commence ta feelin' better," Amanda offered.

"Shore thing," Eli called from the doorway. "It'd be a honor to put up Big Foot Wallace." He grinned. "I heard lots about ya. I hear tell you killed ten Apaches in one settin' with yore rifle, which you call Sweet Lips. Heard lots 'o other stories too. It'd be a pleasure ta hear ya tell about some of your fights."

"Maybe about half of it's true," Wallace responded.

"Now ya hush, Eli. He ain't feelin' fit enough to swap stories with you. Well, Kitty," Amanda said when she had bandaged Wallace's arm. "What do you think 'o my hens?"

"They are fine looking hens," Kitty replied. "I am sure that they will lay lots of eggs."

"Only one thing wrong," Amanda pouted. "We're gonna have to get rid 'o Molasses. Eli done said, either the hens go or Molasses goes. Either way, it shore leaves a soreness in my heart."

"But Molasses, he's — he's so young," Kitty started.

"I know that he ain't full grown, but jest the same he could get a likin' fer chickens."

"Perhaps if you had a rooster like our Gabriel he could protect the hens. Gabriel can fight off chicken hawks," Kitty said proudly.

Amanda listened to Kitty with interest, then said, "Eli done set his mind on it. It's Molasses or the chickens." With downcast eyes, she added, "I need them chickens."

"What will you do with Molasses?" Kitty asked with concern.

Amanda watched Kitty for several moments, then her face brightened. "Kitty, you could take Molasses. Just give him a home and care fer him till he's full grown. Then he can go into the woods and fend fer himself."

"Do you mean it, Amanda?" Kitty asked. She had visions of the pleasure on the younger children's faces when she walked in with Molasses.

"You said your rooster could fight real good. All it would take would be a few taps and ole Molasses would learn his lesson."

Suddenly, Molasses ran through the door, moved up to Kitty, and rubbed against her leg like a kitten. She lifted him up in her arms. "Hello, Molasses!" she said happily, and stroked his fur. The raccoon wriggled about in her arms and pulled on her hair.

"What do you say, Kitty?" Amanda asked.

"Oh yes, Amanda," Kitty cried. "I would be most grateful to have him. My brothers and sisters will be delighted."

"What about yore mama?" Amanda asked.

Kitty looked at Amanda, then back at Molasses. "I'm sure Mama will find a place for him," she answered.

"Molasses," Amanda called happily, "Kitty is your new mistress."

Kitty helped Amanda put breakfast on the table. When she and Wallace had eaten, they thanked the Thompsons and prepared to leave. Wallace had decided to go ahead and make the trip.

Kitty climbed onto Zona, and Amanda put Molasses on the saddle in front of her. Zona began to move about as if she didn't like the additional burden, but Kitty patted her shoulder and soothed her down. Big Foot Wallace watched the pair with amusement. Finally, they said goodbye to the Thompsons and rode away.

8.

Trouble on the Trail

As they rode away from the cabin, the big man
seemed to be forcing himself to sit up straight in the saddle. Kitty studied his face. Though he tried to mask it, he
looked sicker than he had the night before. He knew that
Kitty was concerned.

"It's my aim ta ride to the Injun Territory."

"Indian Territory?" Kitty asked, giving him a startled look.

"Gotta go, Kitty. Time's a runnin' out, and I gotta see
the chiefs."

"Chiefs?" Kitty asked, but all she could think of were
the little Indian people in the Indian Territory.

"I'm going to the Injun Territory," he repeated.

Kitty would have loved to go with him. She wanted
very much to see those little Indian people, but she knew
that she must get home as quickly as possible. William
needed the medicine. She began to ride ahead, and he followed. She studied the trail before them, then looked
back at the wounded man. Neither of them spoke for
some time, and she knew that he must feel very bad.

They were only a few miles down the trail when Kitty heard horses running behind them. She turned around but could not see anyone.

"What did you see, Kitty?" Wallace asked, now very alert.

"I know there are horses coming, but I can't see the riders," she responded.

"Good. If you can't see them, they can't see us. Let's keep it that a way. Take a limb and brush the ground where our horses have been, Kitty," he instructed her. "Then we'll pull off in them bushes and wait 'em out."

Kitty cleared their tracks away with a fallen limb, then pulled the horses into a clump of trees. They waited in silence. Soon three riders emerged on the trail and were clearly visible to her. She recognized them as the same men who had passed her on the trail after Mr. Wallace was assaulted. She looked at him, and the grim, angry expression on his face confirmed her suspicion. They were the same men. She prayed that they would pass without discovering them.

The riders studied each side of the trail, looking for tracks. Kitty watched with fear in her heart as one got down from his horse and observed the area carefully. Suddenly, a flock of birds flew from the tree above her and attracted the rider's attention. She watched as the man on the ground motioned for the others to follow him toward their place of concealment. Kitty saw Big Foot Wallace draw his gun. She also saw perspiration running down his pale face.

Kitty frowned as she thought about the three men approaching their hiding place. She knew that the brave man at her side could handle them when he was well, but he was wounded and feverish. Suddenly, she had an idea. "Wait, don't shoot! Please wait, Mr. Wallace!" she whispered to him.

He gave her a warning glance to be quiet, but Kitty was determined to carry out her idea. She quickly slipped from Zona, taking Molasses with her. Silently, she moved through the woods until she was very near them. "Molasses," she whispered, "I'm going to throw a stick and I want you to bring it back to me."

The raccoon sat up on his hind legs and looked at her with his large brown eyes. His pointed ears stood up very straight through the holes in the red cap. Kitty took the cap off and wondered if he understood her. She picked up a stick and waved it in front of him. Hope surged through her when he began to switch his banded tail.

"Watch the stick, Molasses, and go after it," she whispered, and waved the stick again. When she was sure that she had his attention, she tossed the stick across an open area. She watched Molasses bound after it, and saw one of the men draw his gun. "Don't shoot him," she prayed silently.

"Save yore ammunition, Mel. It's just a coon," the man on the ground called out. "Wallace ain't around here, so we might as well move on down the trail."

"I'm blamed sure that I saw him on the trail a ways back," a bald-headed man on horseback said.

"Well, he ain't here, so let's ride on," Mel responded. "I told you, I shot him in the head and chest. He's dead. We already lost time 'cause you was laid up in the bushes drunk as a skunk."

"You ain't got no reason ta talk. You couldn't even find the message on him."

"There weren't no message on him," the bald man said loudly.

"What if he ain't dead?" the third man asked.

"We'll jest ride ahead on the trail to the Territory, and watch out fer him."

Kitty watched with relief as the men rode away. She joined Mr. Wallace, and they waited long enough for the men to disappear from sight.

"That was good thinking, Kitty. I figger it saved us some gun play and a heap 'o trouble."

"It was Molasses that did it, Mr. Wallace," Kitty responded solemnly.

71

"It was you that put him up to it, Kitty," he said gently. "That raccoon would bring ya a pretty piece of money in the Territory. Some Injun trader would be mighty tickled to have him. They'd pay top money fer that hoss too."

Kitty remained silent for some time. Finally, she asked, "What did those men want, Mr. Wallace?"

"I'm carryin' a message from Sam Houston to the Injun chiefs. It will explain some things to 'em, and prevent them young braves from joining up with the Comanches. Ya see, thar's some folks that's squatting on Injun land in the Nations. They're cheatin' the Injuns outta some of the money owed ta them fer land they ceded to the United States in treaties. On top 'o that, white whiskey peddlers have been a selling whiskey ta the Injuns. It's made 'em pretty riled up at whites. Sam figgers ta get them squatters outta the Territory and get the chiefs to work with the Texans ta put a stop to them whiskey peddlers along the Red River. Them bushwhackers, they're representing some dishonest folks who's making a whole lotta money off 'o that whiskey, and they are part of them that's cheating the Injuns outta some of their money. So long as they can keep the Injuns riled up, ain't likely ta do nothing about the whiskey sellers."

It was just turning dark when Kitty and her companion approached the Garner farm on Blossom Prairie. Rebecca, Kitty's sisters, and two younger brothers were waiting in front of the cabin when they approached. Rebecca closely observed the big man riding behind her daughter, but the children were happily awaiting the arrival of Molasses. Kitty handed Molasses to John Nance and Charlie, then she dismounted.

Rebecca did not scold Kitty as she expected. Instead, she embraced her. "Kitty," she said, "I have been so worried about you."

"I know, Mama, but there was no chill cure in Clarksville, and William had to have it. I didn't want

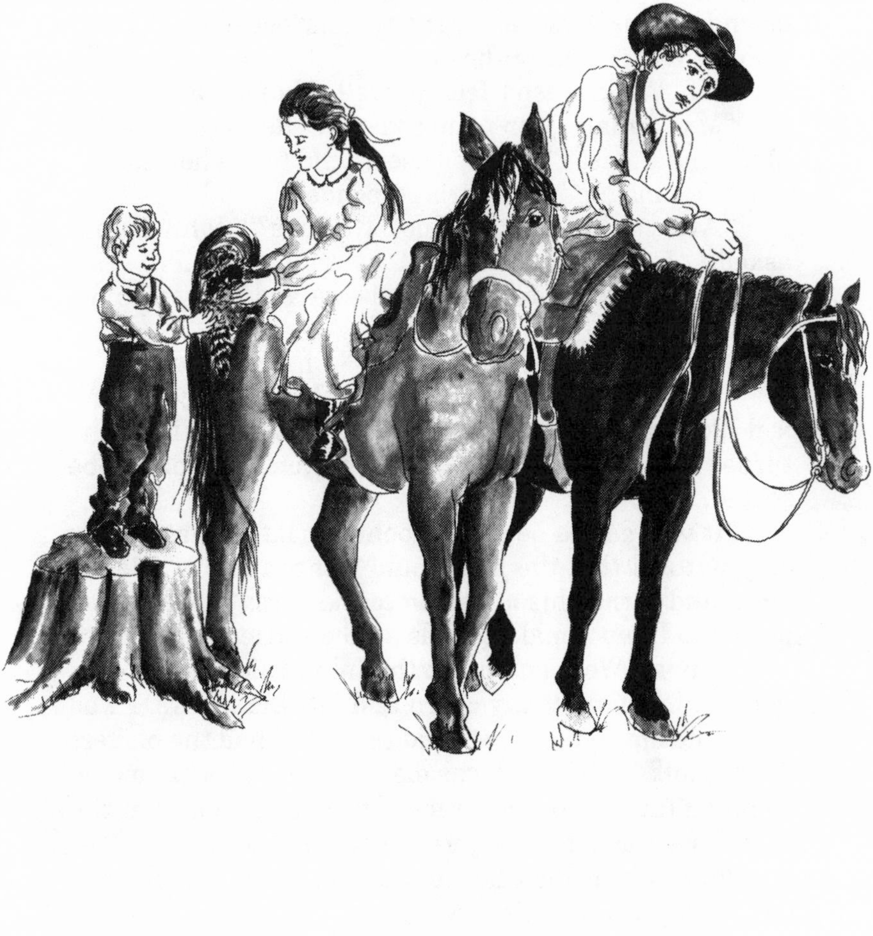

him to die," she said and took the chill cure from her pocket.

"He sure does need it, Kitty, and I am grateful to you." Then Rebecca turned to Mr. Wallace and smiled. "Mama, this is Mr. Big Foot Wallace. He is a friend of Sam Houston."

The big man nodded, wearily. Rebecca smiled and said, "We welcome any friend of Sam Houston, Mr. Wallace. Won't you get down from your horse?"

"Obliged, ma'am," Mr. Wallace responded, and slid down from his horse. Kitty thought he looked even sicker than he had earlier in the day.

"Mr. Wallace isn't feeling well, Mama," Kitty said.

"Mr. Wallace, won't you come in?" Rebecca turned to Mary and Louisa. "Girls, please attend to the horses."

"Yes, ma'am," both girls responded.

"Are you really Big Foot Wallace?" John Nance asked.

"Yep," he said, following Rebecca and Kitty into the cabin.

"Why are you called Big Foot?" Charlie asked.

"Boys," Rebecca scolded them, "Mr. Wallace doesn't feel like answering your questions right now." Then she turned to the visitor. "Mr. Wallace, won't you please be seated?"

"It was gonna be asked sooner or later, ma'am. It's only natural that the lads would want ta know." He sat down and turned his attention to the boys. "There was a big Waco Injun a makin' raids on the settlement where I was a livin'. Well, one night the Injun raided some cabins, then walked to my cabin and left his tracks. I was about the biggest feller around there and had the biggest feet, so folks believed it was me. I proved it wasn't me by stepping into the Injun's tracks and showin' 'em that the Injun's moccasin tracks were too big to be mine."

John Nance and Charlie watched the man with awe, but Kitty grew impatient waiting.

"Mama," she said, "I want to see William."

"Of course," Rebecca replied. "Mr. Wallace, if you will excuse us, we will join you very shortly."

William was still sleeping, and perspiration streamed down his face. "I'll give him some medicine right away," Rebecca said.

Kitty watched as her mother wiped his face, then woke him and gave him some of the dark, bitter liquid. Kitty had carried it in her pocket for two days and was glad to see it used. William saw Kitty standing by his bed and squeezed her hand, then dozed off.

"I have been sponging him with cool water, giving him sassafras tea, and praying. There was nothing else I could do. But with the medicine he will surely get well," Rebecca said cheerfully.

Kitty smiled and patted William on the arm. "I sure am glad, Mama."

"Now tell me about Mr. Wallace, Kitty," her mother requested.

"I found him on the trail to Jefferson, Mama. He had been shot in the arm, and had a large cut on his forehead. I — I took the bullet out of his arm, but he just seems to get sicker."

Rebecca gave her daughter a surprised look. "I see," she said. "He will have to go to bed and stay there for a while. He can sleep in here on John Nance and Charlie's bed."

"He keeps talking about going to see some Indian chiefs in the Indian Territory, Mama. He claims he's on business for Sam Houston. The men who shot him and left him to die were looking for him again this morning. He said that they don't want him to get to the Indians with his message, but he plans to go to see the chiefs," Kitty told her. "I don't think he will stay in bed."

"We'll see about that," Rebecca said, with a determined tilt to her chin.

Much to Kitty's surprise, Mr. Wallace did not argue with Rebecca. He seemed glad to take her orders, and he fell asleep quickly.

75

The rest of the family waited at the table to hear Kitty's story. They listened attentively as she told them what had happened to her since she left Clarksville in search of the chill cure. John Nance and Charlie played with Molasses, while Cleaver sulked in a corner of the room. From time to time he would let out a low growl, and Molasses would make a clicking sound to let him know that he wasn't afraid.

"Mr. Wallace said that Molasses would bring a lot of money in the Indian Territory," Kitty concluded her story.

"Can Molasses stay with us, Mama?" Charlie asked.

Rebecca gave Molasses a suspicious look and said, "I suspect that he has a taste for chickens, son."

"Gabriel won't let him near the chickens, Mama. Not even Cleaver can get to them," Louisa said. Cleaver let out another low growl and all of the children laughed.

As Rebecca spoke, Molasses climbed up into her lap and watched her carefully. Her face softened for a moment, then she put him on the floor. "I guess he will need a home until he is old enough to care for himself."

Molasses stood up straight and switched his long banded tail. All of the children clapped their hands and petted him. Cleaver growled with sullen fury and slipped outside. Molasses seemed to understand that he was accepted — by the children, at least. He crawled to the floor and rolled over several times, which made the children call to him and clap their hands.

Rebecca smiled and pointed her finger at the raccoon. "Sir," she said, "you are very funny while you are young. But when you're older it will be different. You might kill chickens, and you may even bite people." Molasses stood on his hind feet and reached out to her, bringing a new round of laughter from the children.

The next morning, Big Foot Wallace joined the family at the table. Rebecca served him a cup of coffee and some breakfast.

"Kitty, I'll be a leavin' here in a short time," he announced. "I owe it to you that I got this far, and I want ta say that I'm obliged ta you."

It was Rebecca who answered. "Mr. Wallace, you are burning up with fever. The poison from the bullet has spread through your body. If you don't rest and restore your health, you won't be able to travel at all."

The big man wiped perspiration from his forehead and said, "Time's running out, Missus Garner, and I got a mighty important reason to ride into the Nations." Kitty saw his hand tremble as he lifted his coffee cup and added, "Already lost enough time 'cause the bushwhackers got me."

"I have one sick person to attend to, and another won't make that much difference." Rebecca spoke as if she had not heard him. "You're too weak to set your horse and ride such a distance alone, Mr. Wallace."

"Like I said, ma'am, I'm a goin'." He got up from the table. "I reckon I'll saddle my hoss and leave right now."

"Kitty, Mary," Rebecca called, "saddle Mr. Wallace's horse and bring him to the cabin door."

The girls brought the horse to the cabin door and watched as Mr. Wallace walked up to the big stallion. Rebecca and the girls stood back as he attempted to mount the horse. He managed to get one foot into the stirrup, then waited for a moment to gain enough strength to pull his weight up into the saddle. When he was seated, he remained still for several moments while the Garners waited.

Kitty watched and felt very sad. The fever had weakened her friend, and he knew it. He had heard Rebecca's words, and now he was giving them careful thought. The family remained silent as he slipped from the saddle and walked to the cabin. Kitty wondered if he was going to give up, but the determination to go had not left him. She could see it in his eyes.

Rebecca and the children followed him inside the cabin.

"Missus Garner, is there a kinsman of yours — someone I can trust — to make this journey with me? He's gotta have a fast horse and must be prepared to ride with me into the Injun Territory. I wouldn't ask, but I got somethin' mighty important to deliver to them chiefs."

"I am sure that Sam Houston wouldn't have sent you if your mission wasn't important," Rebecca responded. "My cousin Tom is flat of his back with the fever, and most of the men around here are down with it as well. Mr. Wallace," she cautioned him, "you are certainly in no shape to go alone."

Big Foot Wallace removed his hat and rubbed his forehead. "The truth is, ma'am, if I don't meet the Injun chiefs by nightfall with Sam Houston's message, there could be some bloody Injun attacks. There are Comanches wandering about in the Nations right now, and they may hit you again."

Rebecca stood very straight and looked at him with concern. Kitty shuddered at the thought of another Indian attack. "I could send the girls to Clarksville to contact someone," Rebecca offered.

"They'd be too late gettin' back here, ma'am, and I got a deadline to meet," he responded. "Best that I be on my way."

"If the Indians attack again will they kill all of us, Mama?" Mary asked suddenly.

Rebecca turned around with a startled look on her face. She was fully aware of the consequences of another Indian attack, but she looked surprised — as if she had not truly considered that possibility before. She did not answer.

Kitty sat very still, watching and listening. She had a strong desire to go to the Indian Territory. If only Mr. Wallace would take her, and her mother would allow her to go, she would have a chance to find out about the little Indian people.

"I could go with you, Mr. Wallace," Kitty spoke up, and everyone turned to look at her.

78

9.

Ambush in Indian Territory

"**N**o, Kitty," Rebecca responded quickly, "it's too dangerous for you."

"But Mama, someone has to go with him, and Zona is a very fast horse." Kitty saw the answer in her mother's face. Rebecca Garner was not a woman to allow her daughter to ride into known danger.

"Mama, let Kitty go so she can invite the little Indian people to come to Blossom Prairie. The little Indian people will help us survive here," John Nance pleaded with her.

"Please let her go, Mama," Louisa begged. "It may be the only chance we have to invite the little Indian people here."

Rebecca did not respond.

Mr. Wallace watched Kitty for some time, and a solution began to form in his mind. He knew that Rebecca was right. He couldn't make that journey alone. He wasn't altogether sure that he could stay in the saddle all day, the way he was feeling. But Kitty could help him. She could ride through, even if he couldn't. "I believe she could do it, ma'am," he said suddenly. "I'm not sayin' it ain't dangerous, but I know a trail that will keep us out of sight most of the time. The chiefs are friendly, and they will put us up for the night."

Rebecca remained silent while she cleared the breakfast dishes from the table.

"This girl of yours has a lot of courage and common sense to boot, Missus Garner," Mr. Wallace told her. "She struck out on her own to get medicine fer her brother, and got it too. She took a bullet outta my arm. And she and that coon outsmarted them bushwhackers too," he added. "I trust her, ma'am, and I believe that she can help me get the message through."

Rebecca still did not speak.

"I can do it, Mama." Kitty spoke while looking directly at her mother.

Rebecca's face began to soften. Slowly, she turned and addressed Mr. Wallace. "If Kitty helps you to carry out your mission, will it prevent an Indian uprising?"

"Yes, ma'am. I can assure you that the civilized tribes in the Territory will help to keep the Comanches farther away from these parts."

Rebecca stood motionless as she remembered what old Gil had said after the Indian attack on their cabin: *Injuns are Injuns and they bound ta kill whites.*

Big Foot Wallace continued. "Without Sam Houston's message, the civilized tribes may be riled up enough to let the Comanches ride over their lands. A few of the young ones from the Nations may even join up with the Comanches. But the Indians in the Nations, they are civilized tribes, and they trust Sam Houston. If they can read what he's got ta tell 'em. I figger it'll cause 'em to settle them young ones down. Why, they'll likely boot any stray Comanches outta the Territory north of here," he said and added, "I'm weak, ma'am, but I can still sit on my horse and shoot my gun. There's a lot of fight left in me!"

Rebecca studied his face for a moment. "Kitty," she called quietly.

Kitty walked up to her mother. Rebecca embraced her and said, "You will be careful and return to me, won't you?"

"Yes, Mama," she said, hugging her mother tightly.

"We're running short on time, Kitty," Mr. Wallace said.

"I want to know the trail you will be traveling," Rebecca told Mr. Wallace. "If you don't return in a reasonable time I am going after you."

"It's best that you don't know that, ma'am. If the bushwhackers come by here, it'll be best for you. I'll tell Kitty as soon as we're on the trail."

"If Kitty does not return tomorrow, I'm going after her," Rebecca said sternly. "Show me the trail," she commanded.

He observed the determined look on her face and said, "There's a map in my saddlebag. Please get it for me, Kitty." When Kitty brought the saddlebag in, Mr. Wallace spread the map out on the table. "We'll travel this way," he said and looked up at Rebecca. "We'll ride north and cross the Red River here." Kitty and Rebecca watched carefully as he pointed to the map. "About five miles from here, we'll hit the waters of the Kiamichi River. We'll follow it a ways, staying in concealment of trees as much as possible. The chiefs will meet us where the Kiamichi River turns east before emptying into the Red River," he explained. Then he added, "Know the trail well, Kitty. In case I don't make it all the way, you must carry the message."

"Where is the message?" Kitty asked.

"I'll tell you that after we get started," he responded.

"Kitty," Rebecca said slowly, "I want you to take Molasses with you. If the Indian traders will buy him, sell him," she said in a low voice.

Kitty gave her a startled look, then glanced at the rest of the children. Long, sad faces were fixed on Rebecca.

"No, Mama," Louisa cried. "Molasses is so sweet in

his little red cap and his black mask. He will make a wonderful pet for us."

"Please, Mama," John Nance and Charlie pleaded. "Don't sell Molasses."

"I'm sorry, children, but we need the money. We won't have any cotton to sell, and there will be no money coming in. You must understand that Molasses will be different when he grows up. He will steal eggs, melons and corn," Rebecca explained.

As they talked, Molasses paced about on the floor and looked up at Kitty, as if he knew she was leaving. She patted him on the head and watched him reach out to her with his forefeet. She lifted him up and held him close.

"Are you sure we have to sell him, Mama?" Kitty asked.

"Yes, Kitty." Rebecca watched Kitty for several moments before saying, "I also want you to check and see if anyone is interested in buying Zona. If they want her, they can come here and purchase her after you return." Kitty's eyes grew wide as Rebecca spoke. "I don't want to do this, but we must buy supplies. It will give us a chance to survive here." Her eyes misted with tears.

A hurt, angry expression crossed Kitty's face. "Survival!" she said to herself. She started to speak aloud, but Big Foot Wallace stepped forward.

"We need to leave now, Kitty," he said.

Kitty rode away from the cabin with a heavy heart. The family would have to give up Zona and Molasses. She had seen the sad faces of the younger children and the tears in her mother's eyes. She felt burdened with a duty she didn't want to carry out. Zona had always made her mother feel better when she was tired and discouraged. She had good blood lines, and was a treasure for a farm family to own and take pride in. Kitty wished they could keep both animals. She knew, though, that she was traveling to Indian Territory to insure their survival. The children believed that the little Indian people would help them survive on Blossom Prairie. Rebecca felt that money from the sale of Molasses and Zona would purchase supplies and seeds for the coming year. Big Foot Wallace intended to stop an Indian uprising. All three were means of survival.

Molasses sat on the saddle in front of her, holding tightly to the saddle horn. Kitty stopped riding for a moment and turned to look back at the cabin. Wallace stopped beside her.

"Ya shore ya don't want ta go back ta yore folks, girl?" he asked gently.

"No, sir," she responded quickly. She turned Zona around and began to follow Big Foot Wallace toward the trail to the Red River. She knew that he was in a great deal of pain, but he forced himself to sit up straight in the saddle. She could hear him mumbling as he rode.

"I faced danger with some strange looking critters in my day. I done battle beside some trappers that looked half human and some grizzly lookin' rangers. Some 'o them Mexican soldiers weren't too purty neither. But I'll be danged if I ever rode off with a little girl, a storybook, and a half-grown coon." He scratched his head and said, "I reckon I'll jest keep this business ta myself. Yep, that's the best thing ta do with it."

Kitty rode close behind him for several hours. She saw him doze off several times and began to talk to keep him awake.

"Would you like to hear a story, Mr. Wallace?" she asked.

"Reckon I could bear it," he responded.

"This story is about some very little people who lived far, far away and a long time ago. They were called Lilliputians," she explained.

"How little was they?" he asked.

"Maybe this tall," she said as she lifted her hand above the saddle horn.

"Hold on, girl," he protested. "Nobody's that small, so that ain't no true story."

"Of course it isn't," Kitty responded, amused at his reaction. "It's just a make-believe story written by Jonathan Swift."

"Who in tarnation is he?"

"He lived in England a long time ago and wrote a book called *Gulliver's Travels.* My grandfather, Charles Walpole, gave me the book just before he died."

"So this feller jest made up a tale about some little people, did he?"

"Yes, sir, Mr. Wallace." Then Kitty asked abruptly. "Have you ever heard about a race of little Indian people that live in the Indian Territory?"

Big Foot Wallace looked at her strangely. "I heard about them, Kitty, but I ain't never seen hide nor hair 'o one." He grinned, and said, "Maybe they're like them Lilliputians you been talking about — jest make believe."

"Mr. Juber, the peddler said that they do exist," Kitty told him. "I am going to ask about them as soon as we arrive at the Indian camp."

He gave her an odd look and laughed. She was glad to hear him laugh, and thought that he may be feeling better. Soon, though, he began to lean over in the saddle again, and she knew that he was not getting any better.

They rested several times, and each time it was harder for Wallace to get back on his horse. Finally, they stopped on the bank of a small creek and allowed the horses to drink and rest.

"Kitty," the big man called to her. "If I don't make it, I want you to take the message, and ride to the meetin'." He sat quietly for a few moments and looked on all sides while Kitty waited. "It's in the boot on my right foot. Now, you must know how important it is to get that message to them chiefs. The meetin' is to be tonight. I aim to make it, if at all possible. But jest in case worse comes to worse, take the message yourself."

"I will, sir," Kitty assured him.

"It's best that we ride on," he told her and approached his horse. He got his foot into the stirrup, then struggled several moments before he was able to pull his body into the saddle. "I reckon I'll stay put on my hoss until we arrive at the Injun camp," he announced.

They rode north along a well-traveled game trail. After they had ridden for some time, Kitty felt the presence of others on the trail. She began to wonder if they were the little Indian people. She looked back several times but could not see anyone. Finally, she decided that it was her imagination playing tricks on her. The big man riding beside her did not seem to notice, and had not spoken for several hours. She was concerned about him, and wondered if he would be able to ride all the way. She began to ride in front to prevent his being pulled off his horse by limbs.

Kitty heard water lapping against the bank. "We're at the Red River," she announced loudly.

"I reckon we are," he responded. "When we step into that river, we're in the Territory. Ridin's gonna be a might risky from here on out, Kitty. We had best keep a close eye out fer varmints."

"I have a feeling that someone has been following us," Kitty informed him.

"Yep," he responded. "Thar is three of 'em. Waitin' till we get ta a likely place whar they can ambush us, they are."

Kitty gave him a startled look. "Are they the same men who shot you?" she asked, anxiously.

"Most likely," he responded, and took a chew of tobacco. He spoke as if it was just a small annoyance to attend to. "We gonna cross that river and ride at an even pace till we get into a clump 'o bushes. Then, Kitty, we're gonna cut loose and ride hard. I aim ta lose them varmints."

Kitty watched the waters of the Red River grow higher about Zona's legs until it covered the girl's shoes and skirt. Molasses hung tightly to the saddle horn as Kitty rode up the north bank to dry land. Mr. Wallace rode in front of her, and did not seem to be in a hurry. She followed him into a clump of bushes.

"Get ready, girl. We're gonna ride across that gully like the devil is after us fer shore."

Kitty watched as he pulled his rifle from a rawhide bag and placed it on the saddle in front of him. Then he mustered all of his strength, kicked the flanks of his horse, and charged ahead. Zona followed the big stallion, and Kitty gave her free rein as they rode toward a big gully. By the time they had crossed the gully, she could hear other horses galloping behind them. She shuddered to think what would happen if they were caught, but there was no time to panic. They were being pursued at close range by three killers, and she only wanted to lose them. She followed Mr. Wallace into a clump of trees and reined Zona in beside him.

He dismounted there. She started to join him, but he caught the reins of her horse. "I want ya to take the message and keep a goin', Kitty. I'm gonna wait fer 'em and try to stop 'em. I figger, with a little start, you can outrun 'em on that hoss."

"But — but you may be killed," she told him in an alarmed voice.

He didn't answer. Instead, he quickly removed one boot and pulled out an oilcloth pouch. "Take this and my saddlebag, Kitty. Don't stop till ya reach the Injun camp," he commanded her. "When you get thar, show them Injuns that book and ask to see Chief John Ross."

"But Mr. Wallace — " Kitty protested.

"Time's a wastin', girl. Now do as I say, and ride north." With that, he slapped Zona on the back and sent her running.

Kitty rode rapidly along a trail that wove through the trees. She heard shots behind her and knew that Big Foot Wallace had made a stand. She kept going, though, for she knew that he was borrowing time for her. It was up to her now to ride into the Indian camp and deliver Sam Houston's message.

Soon the sound of gun shots ceased, and Kitty shuddered to think what had happened. She had become very fond of Big Foot Wallace. She knew that he was weak, and she was afraid that he had not been able to hold off the three men. Even if she turned back, she wouldn't be able to help him, she thought. She prayed that, by some miracle, he was still alive.

10.

Choctaw

She had traveled some distance before she realized that one of the men was riding behind her. She turned her head and saw that a bearded man with a black hat was gaining on her. Leaning forward, she urged Zona on. "There's a wicked man trying to catch us, Zona. Outrun him, girl! I know that you can do it!" she assured her. "Hang on, Molasses! Hang on for your life!" The raccoon gripped the saddle horn tightly.

Zona put her heart and soul into the race. Kitty glanced back once to see that she had put some distance between her and her pursuer. "Good girl, Zona!" she called to her. "You're the best horse in the whole, whole, world."

The day had moved on and evening shadows were approaching. Zona had been riding hard and needed rest. She began to slow down as she carried her small burdens over the land. Kitty wanted to rest, too, but the man was still riding behind her. She knew that he intended to stop that message from reaching the Indian chiefs, even if he had to kill his horse in the process. He would kill her, too, Kitty thought with horror.

As she entered a clear stretch of land, she turned back to see him within a few yards of her. At the same time she spotted three Indians on a rise just west of her. She observed them briefly, then turned back to watch the bearded man, who was steadily gaining on her. He was watching her so intently that he had not seen the Indians. Panic gripped her as she realized that there were enemies on both sides.

She saw one of the Indians break away from the others and turn south. The bearded man rode alongside Zona and reached out for Kitty, almost pulling her from the saddle. Molasses, sensing danger, snapped at him.

"Leave me alone!" Kitty yelled, striking at him.

"Turn over that pouch!" he demanded. She could hardly hear him over the sound of the horse's hoofs pounding the ground, but he grabbed for her again. Kitty fought with all her might to remain in the saddle. Molasses bit him again, but he would not withdraw his hand. With his other hand, he drew his gun and pointed it at the raccoon. Kitty hit the gun with the saddlebag, causing the bullet to miss Molasses. With an angry twist on his face, he pointed the gun at her. She trembled with fear and prepared for the blast that would end her life.

Suddenly, though, the man yelled out in pain and fell from his saddle. She watched in astonishment, then turned around quickly to see the two Indians in back of her. One had shot an arrow into the bearded man's back.

Now Kitty wondered what was in store for her. As the Indians rode toward her, she readied herself for another attack. But it didn't happen.

"It's time to rest your horse," one of them called gently. Kitty watched him anxiously.

He caught Zona's reins and brought her to a walking gait. They watched Kitty and Molasses curiously, and spoke in their own tongue. One of them pointed to the raccoon's little red cap, and both laughed. Kitty sat quietly in the saddle, pulled Molasses close to her, and observed them carefully. One of them held Zona's reins and led her along. Long, black hair waved in the wind behind them as they rode. They were dressed in cotton trousers but did not wear shirts. Their bodies were not painted like the Indians who attacked the cabin, and one of them spoke English.

"Where are you taking me?" Kitty demanded. She was afraid, very tired, and worried about Big Foot Wallace.

"To a meeting place on the Kiamichi River," the larger Indian responded.

"Oh!" Kitty said with relief. "You must have been sent by the chiefs. Please stop," she pleaded with them.

The Indian pulled on the reins and brought Zona to a halt.

Kitty turned around and pointed behind her. "My friend, Big Foot Wallace, is being ambushed. Would you help him, please?"

"Strong Deer has gone to see about the Big One," the smaller Indian responded, and started Zona again. "I am Small Wolf, and this is Abel, Strong Deer's brother," he informed her.

"I am Kitty Garner," she introduced herself, but continued to watch them carefully.

Soon they approached a small stream and the Indians brought the horses to a halt. "We rest here," Small Wolf announced.

Kitty dismounted and pulled Molasses down with her. The Indians watched as he clung to Kitty's apron. She thought that she detected a grin on their faces when she turned away. She drank from the stream, then sat down on the ground, holding Molasses in her lap. The Indians continued to stand.

Kitty looked at them again with interest. "What kind of Indians are you?" she asked boldly.

"We are Choctaw," Small Wolf answered. He looked at her gently and said, "You are a very brave young girl.

You and the animal fought the bearded white man with courage." He pointed south, and said, "Look!"

Kitty saw dust kicked up on the trail. She stood up and waited anxiously. An Indian rode over the hill, and behind him was Big Foot Wallace. He was leaning low in the saddle, but he was alive.

"He is alive!" Kitty called excitedly. "Big Foot Wallace is alive!"

He rode up to her and grinned. "Thought I was a goner, didn't ya, Kitty?"

"I knew that if anyone could make it, you could, sir," she responded happily. "What happened to the other two men?"

"Had to do in both of 'em," he reported solemnly. "I am mighty grateful ta this feller fer helping me on my hoss." He turned toward the Indian and offered his hand. He looked toward the sky, and turned to Kitty again. "I reckon it would be best if ya was to turn over the pouch and the saddlebag to me."

"Of course," Kitty said.

"It will soon be dark, so we'd best ride on," he informed the others.

Both Indians looked at him with respect and offered him the lead position.

Kitty and Big Foot Wallace rode in front, while the Indians followed. She felt that they were safe now, and began to relax. She knew that Mr. Wallace did not feel like talking, and the three Indians riding behind them talked in their own language. She was left with her own thoughts.

Zona and Molasses had helped to save her life, and her heart ached at the thought of losing them. She patted Zona on the shoulder, leaned over and whispered to her, "About the only hope I have of keeping you and Molasses is those little Indian people. I sure do hope they are real." She wanted desperately to believe that the little Indian people were real, for she thought they would surely help her.

Her family had been on Blossom Prairie for about seven months and they had often wondered about this Indian Territory, just fourteen miles north of them. Now that she had the opportunity, she began to observe her surroundings so that she could give a report to the rest of the family. The area didn't look all that different from the land in Red River County. She saw many post oak, black jack oak, as well as hickory and pecan trees. There were some beautiful pine trees as well.

They rode through wooded areas and across some prairie land with tall grass sweeping up and dancing in the wind. Then the land became gently rolling and hilly in spots. She spotted deer, wild turkey, and a variety of birds. Squirrels and rabbits were in abundance all about them.

In the fading light of evening, and much to her surprise, Kitty spotted a farm house in the distance. She wondered who lived there, for she had always heard that Indians lived in tepees.

Two of the Indians rode up alongside Big Foot Wallace, and the big man brought his horse to a halt. The Indians spoke in the Choctaw tongue, and Wallace responded in kind. As they talked, the smaller Indian rode beside Kitty. "It is time for these brothers to return home. Their father has many farm chores for them to do."

Kitty gave him a startled look, and he explained. "They live in that farm house over there."

"But — but," Kitty started.

"Did you think that all Indians live in tepees, or out in the open?" He smiled in a humorless way.

"Yes," Kitty replied honestly.

"Some of the full-bloods in the Choctaw Nation do live in tepees. But many of us live in houses and work the land just as the whites do."

"I did not know that," Kitty told him.

"We also wear the citizens' dress, and we go to school," he said. "There are five civilized tribes in what you call the Indian Territory. Each of the civilized tribes lives in its own special area, called a nation. We have a government much like your own. Our government works well until we have to deal with untrustworthy Indian agents, intruders on our land, and white whiskey traders on our borders. You see, we have courts and lawmen, but our laws do not apply to the whites who intrude on our land." He spoke with a grim twist to his mouth.

Kitty listened with fascination. She knew that this special meeting had something to do with Indian agents, intruders, and the whiskey traders. "Have your people always lived here?" she asked.

"No," he replied. "They came from the same states that many of you Texans migrated from. The difference is that my people and the other civilized tribes were brought here to this land, you call Indian Territory, by military troops. Your people came on their own, and chose the land they wished to settle on. They are free to move to another place if they like."

"Why did the military troops move your people?" Kitty asked.

"My people owned fine farms and plantations, but the whites who started coming wanted their rich land." There was a far-away look in his eyes as he continued. "It will happen again," he said. "Perhaps not in my lifetime, but surely it will happen again. There will be those who will covet this land as they did the land in the southern states."

Kitty looked at him sadly. "I hope that you are wrong," she said.

The stern look on his face softened.

"Small Wolf," she asked, "do you know about the little Indian people?"

A slow grin crossed his face. "Why do you ask about the little Indian people?"

"Mr. Juber, a peddler, told us about them. Our cotton crop failed because of the heavy rains, and Mama is worried about our survival on Blossom Prairie. She . . . she wants me to sell Molasses and see about selling Zona as well. I don't want to sell them," Kitty explained. "The smaller children have to work hard and we have few visitors. They need Molasses to play with. They need to remember a happy childhood, like Mama does. Mama needs Zona, and I do. I thought that if the little Indian people are real, they may be able to help."

"I will send you to one who will tell you about them," Small Wolf said thoughtfully.

Kitty wanted to ask him more, but he pulled the reins of his horse and began to ride behind hers.

Darkness quickly covered the land. Small Wolf had fallen into silence, and Kitty wished that their journey would end. She missed her family, Molasses was very restless, and she was hungry. At last she saw the light of campfires ahead of them, and knew they were approaching the meeting place. Small Wolf went ahead to announce their arrival.

11.

Meeting on the Kiamichi River

Kitty rode beside Big Foot Wallace as they entered the camp. She knew that he was in pain, but he sat straight in the saddle. There was a fire by the bank of the river, and women were cooking over it. Kitty could see several important looking men sitting together in straight-back chairs and on the ground. She decided that they must be the chiefs and other important leaders. Some of them were dressed as white men, with tall, black hats and black vests. Several were dressed as one would expect an Indian to dress, with buckskin trousers and a band about their long, black hair. One man, wearing very little clothing, sat stoically on the ground and looked very angry. Some of the others smoked pipes as they studied the two figures on horseback.

Kitty observed the campsite with wide-eyed interest. Some mules and horses were hobbled nearby, and there were several covered wagons and some tents. Children were playing about the camp, but they stopped their game to watch the strangers ride in. There were also many dogs around, and they began to bark at Molasses.

He watched them fearfully and clung to Kitty, until several of the men called them off. Kitty's eyes scanned the people with great curiosity, for they did not resemble the Indians who attacked them on Blossom Prairie.

Big Foot Wallace stopped in front of the chiefs, took his saddlebag, and dismounted with great effort. Kitty slipped from Zona and stood beside him. She noticed that Small Wolf stood behind one of the men sitting with the chiefs and waved to him.

A tall, straight man stood up and lifted his arm. Kitty noticed that his skin was very fair, and he had deep blue eyes. "Welcome," he greeted them.

"My name's Will Wallace," her friend said. "This little lady is Kitty Garner. She lives over in Red River County on Blossom Prairie. Helped me ta get here, she did. I reckon that she owns the book that's gonna show me to be from Senator Sam Houston." The chiefs watched Kitty with interest. Then Big Foot Wallace took the book, *Oliver Twist,* from his saddlebag and handed it to the chief for inspection.

The chief accepted the book and smiled. "Welcome friend of the Raven. I am John Ross, a chief of the Cherokees."

Big Foot Wallace tilted his hat and said, "I reckon you're the one to get the message from Senator Houston."

Chief John Ross nodded, but the angry looking man on the ground grunted.

Kitty watched as Wallace handed the chief the oil skin pouch. Then he turned to her. "Kitty, we'd best make ourselves scarce while the chiefs mull over this message."

"We are most grateful to you, Mr. Wallace, and to you, Kitty. I know that it has been difficult for you to get the message here. But the Raven would only select the most worthy man for such a mission. Now Small Wolf will see to your needs," Chief John Ross said in an air of dismissal. "As you said, we have a very important matter to settle."

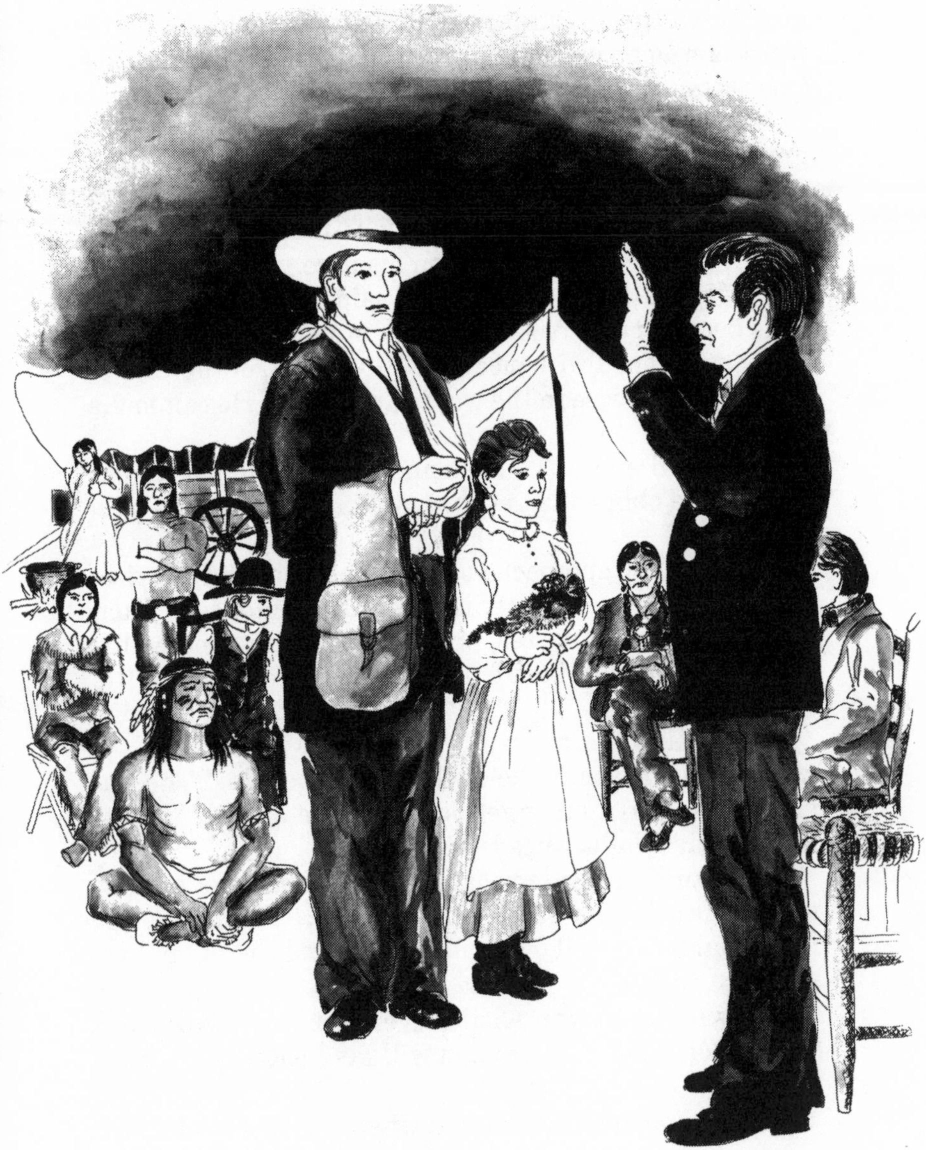

Small Wolf stepped from behind the chair of a tall man dressed in citizens' clothing. "I would like you to meet my father, Running Deer. He is not a chief, but his word is much respected among the Choctaws and the Cherokees."

Both Kitty and Big Foot Wallace extended their greetings to him. Then Small Wolf led them toward a small, silver-haired man who sat cross-legged before a tent on the outer edge of the campsite. He looked to be very old and wore spectacles on his nose.

"Mr. Wallace," Small Wolf said, "I know that you have been very ill. You are a very brave man and should not be weakened with sickness. Silver Fox, of the Cherokee Nation, is wise in the ways of medicine. He can make you well."

"I heard about the medicine yore people got, Small Wolf. I'd be obliged ta get shed 'o this fever, and the pain in my arm."

When they approached him the old man did not rise. He only looked up and studied their faces intensely. Then his eyes fell on Molasses, and a gentle smile crossed his face. "It is good to be a friend to those creatures of the woods," he said.

"I'm Kitty Garner, sir," Kitty spoke quickly. "I — I want to learn about the little Indian people." The old man gave her a strange look, but she added, "First, though, Mr. Wallace needs some help."

He studied her face carefully for a moment, then turned his attention to Big Foot Wallace. "You are ill, but I will make you well," he said and offered the big man a seat next to him.

"I will leave you with Silver Fox, Mr. Wallace." Small Wolf said. "The women will give Kitty something to eat."

Kitty had smelled the food when she entered the Indian camp and had hoped that they would offer her food. As she approached the fire, the women smiled warmly, and Kitty smiled back. They stood over iron pots and stirred the food with wooden spoons as it bubbled up. A large chunk of venison was roasting over the fire.

"If you will sit on the ground, the women will get you some food. You may feed the raccoon as well," Small Wolf instructed her.

She sat down on the ground, and Small Wolf sat down beside her. One of the women, who was dressed in an ankle-length dress made of gingham, picked up a large plate and pointed to one of the pots.

"She wants to know if you would like the food from that pot. It is *walakshi,* or dumplings made of corn meal and boiled in water that is flavored with grape juice."

"Yes," Kitty said, and added, "I would also like some venison."

She waited while Small Wolf spoke to the woman in the Choctaw tongue. The woman filled the plate with the dumplings and a large piece of venison. She also gave Kitty a gourd cup filled with water. She filled a smaller plate for Molasses, and gave him some water.

The women stopped working and watched Molasses eat. The children gathered around to watch him too. Kitty was amused to see him dip each piece of food in the gourd of water before putting it into his mouth. The women and children laughed loudly each time he ate a bite of food.

"What do you think of my people, Kitty?" Small Wolf asked.

"They are not as I expected them to be," she responded, and looked about her.

"How did you expect them to be?"

"Like . . . like the Indians who attacked our farm. They looked wicked and cruel, and I feared them. These people are very friendly. There is only one who looks like the others. He is wearing little clothing and sits with the chiefs."

"He is a Comanche," Little Wolf responded, and his face hardened. "There is some discontent among some of the young men and he wishes to incite them to follow his

99

lead to fight the whites." He rose and said, "It is time I joined my father. Feel free to walk about the camp when you have finished eating. Silver Fox will soon be ready to speak with you."

Kitty could see the chiefs huddled together across the way, hotly debating the message sent by Senator Sam Houston. She hoped that they would end any thoughts of an Indian uprising. She could hear the sound of the Comanche's voice, and knew that he was not happy with Sam Houston's message.

When she had eaten, she thanked the women. Several of the children walked up and patted Molasses on the head, and he responded by rolling over for them. Finally, Kitty picked him up, waved to the women and children, and walked toward Silver Fox's tent.

Big Foot Wallace was lying on a blanket in front of the tent. A piece of animal skin had been pressed over the bullet wound in his arm. Another piece of skin, saturated with yellow oil, covered his forehead. The big man seemed to be sleeping soundly.

"Hello!" Kitty called at Silver Fox's tent door.

"You may come in," Silver Fox invited her.

Kitty opened the tent flap and walked in. The interior was illuminated by candlelight.

"Your friend is sleeping now. When he awakes the fever will be gone," Silver Fox assured her.

"I am very glad, Mr. Silver Fox," Kitty said with relief. "He has been in much pain."

"The pain will go with a cup of tea I have for him," the old man told her. "You may sit down. I have something to attend to, then I will join you." With that he left the tent.

Kitty sat down on a skin that was spread out on the floor. Molasses lay down for a nap, leaving her to explore the tent. She saw several books lying on the tent floor and began to look through them. *Oliver Twist* was on the bottom of the stack. She opened it up and saw a torn page. There was also another page that her brother Charlie had marked. Kitty realized that it was the book Sam Houston had borrowed from her. Silver Fox must be Sam Houston's old Indian friend who liked storybooks. Kitty smiled. It seemed so long ago since they had met Sam Houston just north of the Red River in Arkansas.

She picked up two newspapers. One was the *The Choctaw Intelligencer,* and the other, written partly in English, was *The Cherokee Advocate.* She selected another book which she found interesting. It was written in a strange language, but there were many drawings of tiny Indian men in full Indian dress. Suddenly, happy awareness came over Kitty and she gasped, "The little people!" Her heart beat faster, and she quickly scanned the rest of the book. There were pictures of plants underneath the figures of the little Indian people.

Kitty was so intent in looking through the book that she did not hear anyone enter the tent. Her whole body tensed in anticipation as she became aware of a small figure behind her. Molasses stirred and crawled toward Kitty. She desperately wanted to see who was there, but she did not turn around. She believed that it was one of the little Indian people, and was afraid it would become frightened and disappear.

Kitty could wait no longer. Slowly she turned around to peer into the face of a small person. "Why — you aren't one of the little people. You're just a little girl." Disappointment showed on Kitty's face as she observed an Indian girl about her age.

The girl did not speak, but moved toward Silver Fox as he made a sudden appearance in the tent.

"This is Lily," he said, patting the little girl on the head. "She wants me to tell you that you are welcome to share her bed tonight."

"Thank you, Lily," Kitty said. The little girl turned to Silver Fox with a puzzled expression.

He spoke to Lily in another language, and she left the tent.

"It will be a happy memory for her," he told Kitty

101

when Lily left the tent. "I see that you have an interest in the 'little people.' " He saw the open book on her lap.

"I have heard about the little Indian people, sir, and I want to know if they truly exist. If they do, I want to see some of them. Would you please tell me about them?" He sat down beside her. "They are little like the Lilliputians," he responded.

"Do you know about the Lilliputians?" she asked in wonderment.

"I have read some of Jonathan Swift's work," he said with a certain air of pride.

"Is this an Indian storybook?" she asked, pointing to the book. "The Lilliputians are only make-believe people."

"It is a book that I am writing. The Creeks, Choctaws, Chickasaws, and Seminoles sometimes speak of a race of very small human beings, Kitty. They are said to be invisible most of the time. But sometimes children and medicine men are able to see them. I have attempted to draw some of the little people as they are described to me. I also draw pictures of medicinal plants," he said and added, "The little people are said to have knowledge of these plants."

"Do you believe they really exist?" Kitty asked anxiously.

"I believe in many things," he said. "Many white people believe in a race of little people. There are stories of elves and leprechauns that go way back in your own history. Is it so strange that the Indian should have such a similar culture?"

"No," Kitty replied. She sat very still and listened intently as he spoke.

"Why do you wish to see the little people, Kitty?" he asked.

"We lost our cotton crop due to floods, and we don't have enough money for next year's supplies. Mama wants me to sell Molasses and our horse, Zona," she said. "She really doesn't want to sell them, but she feels she

102

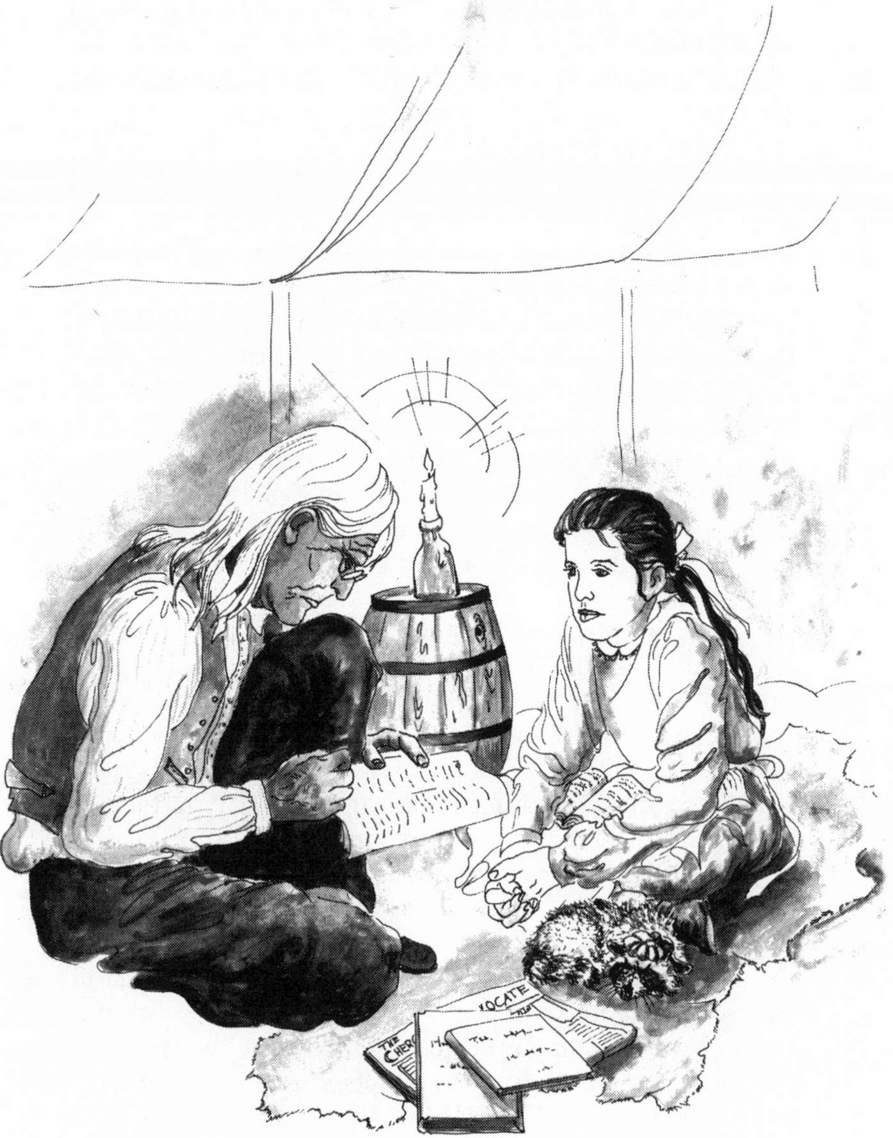

must. The younger children strongly believe in the little people, and feel that they can help us."

"I see," he responded. "How many children are in your family, Kitty?"

"There are six of us in all. Charlie, my youngest brother, is only four years old."

"And your father?"

"Papa passed away while we still lived in Tennessee," she said.

Silver Fox looked at her thoughtfully for a moment, then said gently, "You have had a long journey, and it is getting late. You may leave the raccoon here. If the little people appear, it will be very late at night. Lily will be alerted and wake you."

One of the women placed a blanket on the ground for Kitty and Lily to sleep on. She could still hear the chiefs talking and knew that they had not reached an agreement. Kitty was tired and there had been so much excitement throughout the day, but she could not fall asleep right away.

She prayed that she would not have to sell Molasses and Zona. She had seen the pleasure on the younger children's faces when they played with Molasses. Even when they were older, the memories of their happy days with him would survive. Her mother's memories of Ginger survived, and Zona reminded her of her dream for her family. She thought about the farm on Blossom Prairie way into the night, and she thought about the meaning of the word "survival." The little Indian people occupied her thoughts as well.

Kitty awoke the next morning to the noisy activity of the camp. She looked about for Lily, but the girl was not there. Two women were cooking food over the fire, but she realized that many of the people and some of the wagons were missing. Chief John Ross and Small Wolf's father sat quietly talking together, and she was glad to see that the Comanche was gone. He was the only one of the Indians who frightened her.

As she got up, she saw Big Foot Wallace and Silver Fox walking toward her. Silver Fox was carrying Molasses, and Mr. Wallace was leading Zona. Mr. Wallace walked straight, and his face did not show the pain of the previous day.

"How do you feel?" she asked her friend.

"Finely," he responded. "I mean it too. Silver Fox kept his word and fixed me up."

"I am so glad," Kitty said.

"I saw Lily early this morning, Kitty. She told me that the little people did not appear last night," Silver Fox told her.

"I know." The disappointment showed on Kitty's face.

"Yore ma asked ya to see about sellin' these animals, Kitty," Wallace reminded her, but Kitty was not listening.

Suddenly, she turned to Silver Fox. "Have you ever seen the little Indian people?" she asked anxiously.

"No," he answered, "but I believe they are there for some people to see."

"If you have never seen them yourself, how can you be sure they exist?" Kitty challenged him sharply.

"I cannot see the wind, yet it is there," he responded gently.

Kitty watched him thoughtfully for several moments, while Big Foot Wallace and Small Wolf waited. "Is . . . is that like faith, sir?" she asked. Her eyes shined with the excitement of a new discovery.

"I would say so, Kitty," Silver Fox replied, watching her expression.

"Kitty," Small Wolf said, "the trader would like to look at Zona, and he will surely make a good offer for her. He has said that he will be glad to buy Molasses too."

Kitty stroked Zona's mane and patted Molasses on the head. She had seen the men looking at Zona and knew that they admired her. She could get a good price for Zona, and there would be enough money to purchase seeds and supplies for the coming year. Kitty looked toward the trader, then stroked Zona again. The decision to sell the animals weighed heavy on her mind, and she stood quietly for several moments. Then she quickly turned, took Zona's reins, and led her toward the trader. Small Wolf, Silver Fox, and Big Foot Wallace watched as she talked to the trader, but they could not hear her. Therefore, they were surprised to see her turn Zona about and lead her toward them.

"I won't be selling Molasses or Zona," Kitty announced, as if she had made a definite decision. "I intend to take them back to Blossom Prairie with me."

"Are ya shore about that, Kitty?" Big Foot Wallace asked with a puzzled expression.

"Yes, sir," Kitty said and lifted her chin up high. "We're going to survive on Blossom Prairie, Mr. Wallace. I have faith that we will. But dreams and happy memories from our childhood need to survive too."

"Would you please explain why you made this decision, Kitty?" Silver Fox asked as he studied her face.

"Next year is like the wind. I can't see it, yet I believe that we will survive the winter and plant our crops all over again. I believe that there is more to surviving than food and seeds. I . . . I guess that believing, remembering, and dreaming is a part of what survival is all about," Kitty concluded.

Silver Fox looked at her long and thoughtfully. "You are a wise young lady, and it has been an honor to meet you, Kitty," he said. "Perhaps you will visit us in the Cherokee Nation sometime."

Kitty smiled and said, "I would like that, sir."

"If that's the way of it, Kitty, I'll ask ya ta collect that coon and yore storybook. Best we be on our way back to yore prairie home," Wallace said with a smile. He shook hands with Small Wolf. "I'm obliged to ya," the big man said.

"My people, the Choctaws, and the other civilized

tribes are most grateful to you, and to Kitty. The Raven is much respected among all our people. With your help, he sent his word that all matters will be attended to, and much trouble has been prevented. The Comanches will find trouble elsewhere."

"I'm mighty glad ta hear that," Wallace said.

12.

Blossom Prairie

Kitty and Big Foot Wallace returned from the Indian Territory. The big man extended his thanks to Kitty and Rebecca, then said goodbye to the Garner family.

Kitty was left to face her mother. She had disobeyed Rebecca, but felt strongly that she had done the right thing in not selling the animals. She held her chin high and approached her mother. Rebecca listened carefully as she explained why she had not sold Molasses and Zona.

"Our family traveled all the way from Tennessee to Texas, yet we had never seen Blossom Prairie. But Mama, we believed there would be good land, and that we could start a farm. We lived through an Indian attack and a terrible storm. And William is recovering from prairie fever. Gabriel showed up on the farm when we needed a rooster."

When Rebecca did not speak, Kitty continued. "Zona is a link with your past in Tennessee. You may work all day plowing, but when you stroke Zona's mane the weariness seems to leave you. We all love her and she repre-

108

sents your dream for our future. All of us work hard, and sometimes we must face danger, but Molasses makes us laugh. We need to make some happy Texas memories that will survive all of us, and we must have more faith, Mama."

"I don't want to part with Zona or Molasses, but we must think of our future, our survival," her mother said. "You know, Kitty, that I want all of you to remember our home as being happy. But we can't always have what we want. It is sometimes necessary to make sacrifices."

"You will always make our home happy, Mama, and I believe we will make it just fine," Kitty assured her.

Rebecca smiled and said, "We certainly will." But she continued to watch Kitty, for she knew that Kitty had something else to say.

"Mama, I know that we must have the seeds and supplies. If we don't find another way, we can still sell Zona to the Indian trader. He will be in Fort Towson the first week in February. If you still feel that we must sell Zona, William can take her there."

Even before Kitty finished talking, she saw tears roll down her mother's cheeks. "Kitty, how did you get so wise?" she asked, and hugged her daughter tightly.

"I had a good teacher, Mama," Kitty replied.

"I'm glad you didn't sell them, Kitty. As you said, we do need to have more faith. Perhaps something will happen before February and we can keep both of them. In the meantime, we will enjoy them."

The threat of Indian attacks passed and William recovered his full health. Fall appeared and gave the trees a beautiful change of colors. Kitty liked to walk beneath the large red oak trees and see the amber and gold colors as the sun filtered through the boughs. A brisk coolness stirred in the air, and the Garners were reminded of Tennessee. But they talked less and less of their former home, and considered themselves to be Texans.

Kitty loved the prairie even more than before. She still had faith that something would happen so that they would not have to sell Zona. There was less work to do, and the children had more time to play. Molasses gave them many amusing moments, and Kitty was happy to see Rebecca take time to ride Zona.

The flour and salt supply was very low, and there was no sugar or coffee. But the storm cellar still held a good supply of dried vegetables and fruit. The woods abounded in venison, rabbits, and squirrels, which made good stews. The family was grateful for what they had, and they prayed that somehow they would manage without selling Zona.

In early December, Mr. Juber returned to the farm on his way to the Indian Territory. All the family stopped working and waited for him to stop his mule in front of the cabin.

"Hello, Mr. Juber," the children called excitedly.

"Won't you stop and share a meal with us, Mr. Juber?" Rebecca invited him.

"No, ma'am. I'm obliged to ya, but I want to get on with my tradin' in the Injun Nations. I jest stopped by to leave this letter fer ya. The stagecoach driver give it ta me in Clarksville," he explained, and handed Rebecca a letter.

"Thank you, Mr. Juber," Rebecca said and looked at the letter with interest.

"I reckon I'll be on my way, unless ya got some tradin' to do," he said and waited.

"Sorry, Mr. Juber, but we don't have money for trading," Rebecca responded.

He nodded and called out to his mule. "I'll stop by on my way back," he said and waved goodbye to the children.

Rebecca opened the letter carefully while the children waited impatiently.

"It's a letter from Senator Sam Houston, children," Rebecca said happily.

"What does it say, Mama?" the children asked anxiously.

"Dear Rebecca," their mother started, "I want to extend my thanks to your daughter, Kitty, for services rendered to Texas and the nation. I received a report from our Indian friends north of the Red River. Big Foot Wallace carried out an important mission that helped to resolve differences between us and our friends. Mr. Wallace wrote me, too, and assured me that he could not have made the trip without Kitty's help. Texas and the nation are grateful to Kitty Garner for services rendered.

"The President of the United States would also like to extend his appreciation to Kitty, and I include his letter. You have reason to be proud, Rebecca. Sincerely, your friend, Sam Houston."

Kitty's mouth dropped open as she stood in astonishment. She had listened intently as her mother read Sam Houston's letter, but she could not move when her mother handed her the president's letter.

"Kitty," Rebecca called to her, "don't you understand? It's a letter from the president of the United States of America."

Finally, Kitty moved to accept the letter.

"I have an idea, Kitty," Rebecca said. "Why don't you open the letter on Christmas Eve? You can read it to all of us and it will be a special Christmas present."

"That's a good idea, Mama," Kitty said. Excitement shined in her eyes as she held the letter up and inspected it. "It will be just like President Filmore has come to spend Christmas with us."

As Christmas drew near, the children looked forward to celebrating it. But they had reason to be very excited about an event that happened the day before Christmas. They woke early one frosty morning to hear Cleaver barking and Gabriel crowing. All of them went outside to see what was disturbing them. Not far from the cabin, they saw some barrels and sacks stacked up in a pile. William carried his rifle and approached quietly.

The rest of the family waited near the cabin while he looked about the area.

"It's food stuff, Mama. There's flour, sugar, coffee, salt, and some seed for next year's crop," he yelled happily.

The rest of the family ran toward him and began to look in wonderment at the items stacked on the ground.

"Where did they come from?" John Nance asked.

"I don't know," his mother responded. She turned to William, who was investigating some wagon tracks leading into the woods.

"Maybe the little Indian people brought them," John Nance said, looking north.

"Yes, Mama," Louisa said, "it must have been the little Indian people!"

"Whoever they are, they're out of sight now," William announced.

"Kitty, you said you didn't see the little Indian people, but do you believe in them?" Mary asked.

"I didn't see the little Indian people, but I can't see the wind, either," Kitty answered quietly, and gave her mother a knowing look.

"Look, Mama," William called. "The sign on this flour barrel has a Choctaw symbol on it."

"The supplies *did* come from the little Indian people!" Louisa announced, and turned to her mother for reassurance. "Didn't they, Mama?"

"Children, I think we have some very good neighbors just across the Red River," their mother said happily.

"The little Indian people!" John Nance and Charlie said.

"Good neighbors," Rebecca repeated. "Now we must hurry and take the supplies inside the cabin. Today is Christmas Eve and we need to select a tree to trim for Christmas."

"Do you know what this means, Mama?" Kitty asked excitedly.

"Yes, Kitty. Zona will always belong to our family."

112

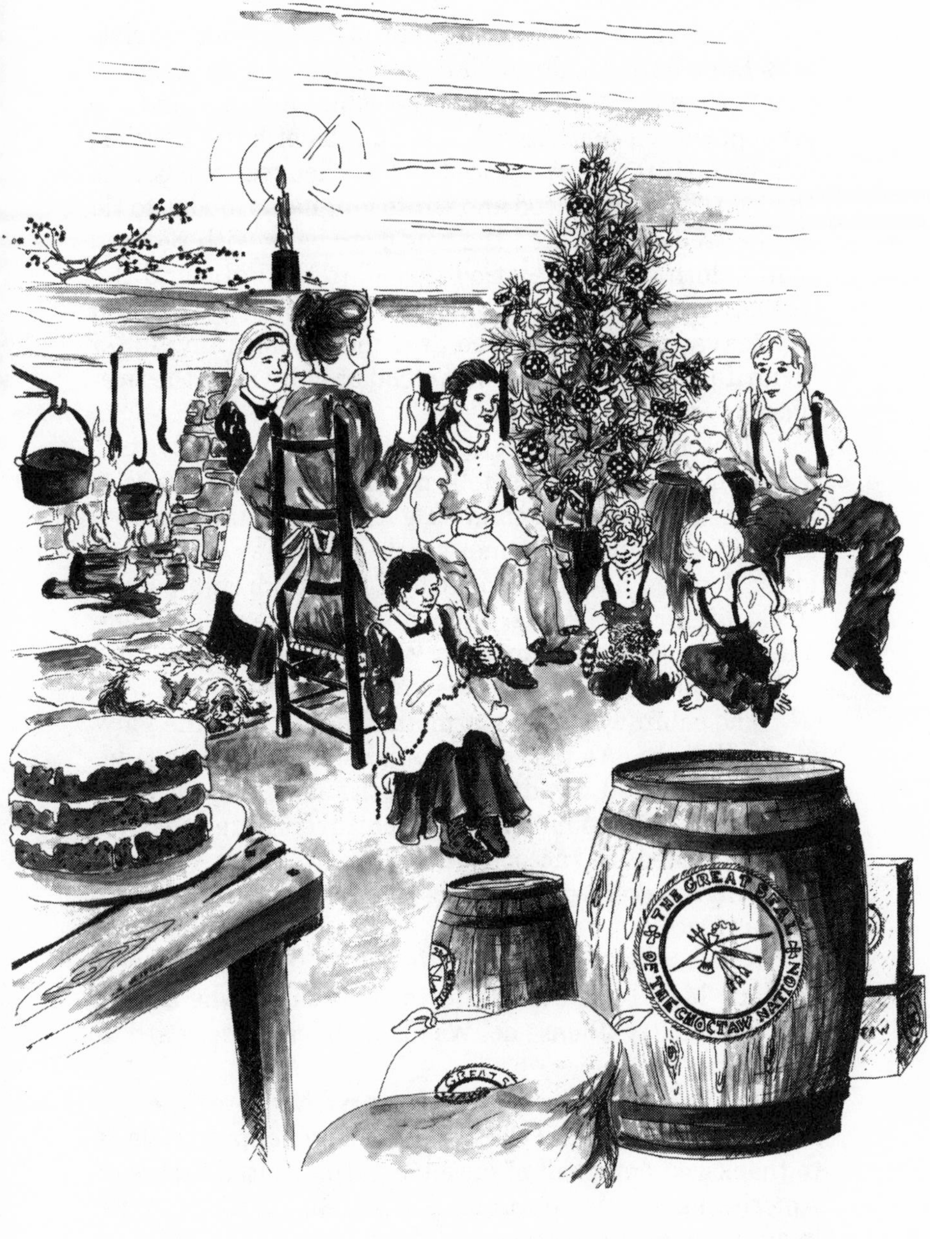
THE GREAT SEAL OF THE CHOCTAW NATION

Kitty embraced her mother and they laughed out loud.

Everyone helped to make preparations for Christmas Eve. William, John Nance, and Charlie cut a small pine tree and placed it inside the cabin. Rebecca and the girls gathered bois d'arc balls, boughs of holly berries, and beautiful amber colored red oak leaves to decorate the tree. They made red and white gingham ribbons to tie on the tree and covered the bois d'arc balls with red and white cloth. Then they tied thread to the balls and the dry leaves, and hung the colorful balls, holly berries, and dry leaves to the pine tree branches. Soon they had a beautiful Christmas tree that stood proudly near the fireplace.

Rebecca made a spice cake for the Christmas Eve celebration, and the spicy smells permeated the air. As soon as it was dark, they lit candles, gathered around the tree, and began to sing Christmas carols. Next they exchanged gifts. Rebecca had knitted each of the children a pair of stockings for Christmas. Kitty and her sisters had made a new bonnet for their mother. William, John Nance, and Charlie had made some wooden candle holders.

The cabin was very warm and beautiful in the glow of candlelight. As they sat around the Christmas tree, Molasses pulled a red ball from the tree and rolled it around on the floor. All of the children laughed, and Charlie pulled the raccoon onto his lap. Cleaver, who had grudgingly accepted Molasses, stretched out lazily near the fireplace.

Kitty took the president's letter from her apron pocket. "May I read the letter now, Mama?" she asked.

"Yes, Kitty. Please do. We have all looked forward to hearing it."

Kitty opened it quickly and cleared her throat before beginning. "Dear Miss Garner — It is my happy privilege to thank you on behalf of myself and the United States of America for heroic efforts in assisting Mr. Wallace to deliver an important message to Chief John Ross. Signed —

Millard Filmore, President of the United States (1852)."

"I am very proud of you, Kitty!" Rebecca said. "The letter is a wonderful Christmas present."

"I will cherish and remember this letter through all my days on Blossom Prairie," Kitty said thoughtfully as she folded the letter. "But I cherish the warmth and love of our family more," she announced, and was pleased to see her mother smile happily.

"Tell us about the special dream Zona causes you to think of, Mama," John Nance requested.

"She reminds me of the home my family had in Tennessee and in North Carolina. My father always kept fine horses, and Zona is of the same blood lines." Suddenly, Rebecca turned to him and said, "One day you will have a large house on Blossom Prairie similar to your Grandpa Charlie's house. You will have fine horses, and many acres of this land will belong to you. Some of your children will become important to Texas and to the nation."

"Will we survive, Mama?" Charlie asked.

"Yes, son, we will survive. And many happy memories will survive with us," Rebecca said, and she smiled at Kitty.

Historical Notes

Chapter 1: **Indian Attack**

The Garner family traveled from Tennessee to Texas in 1851, built a cabin, and started a farm on Blossom Prairie. Just fourteen miles north of them, across the Red River, was the vast Indian Territory.

The Choctaw, Creek, Seminole, Cherokee, and Chickasaw Indians were forcibly moved to this area between 1830 and 1843, and on June 30, 1834, the federal government set aside the land as Indian country (later known as Indian Territory). In 1866 the western half of Indian Territory was ceded to the United States, which opened part of it to white settlement in 1889. This portion became the Territory of Oklahoma in 1890, and eventually emcompassed all the lands ceded in 1866. The two territories were united and admitted to the Union as the state of Oklahoma in 1907.

The civilized Indians in the Territory gave their white Texas neighbors little trouble. But occasionally, wandering bands of Comanches or Kiowas raided farms of the white settlers in northeast Texas and stole cattle and horses.

Chapter 2: **The Peddler**

In the mid-1800s the prairie was a lonely place where life brought hard work and few visitors. A visit from a peddler was most welcome, for he brought much news of other people and places with him.

Cock fights were legal during the 1800s and occurred in various places.

117

Some of the Choctaw, Creek, Seminole, and Chickasaw Indians spoke of a race of little Indian people.

Chapter 3: **The Dark Wind**

Tornadoes were frequent along the Red River Valley, especially in the spring.

Centuries ago, methods of preserving food were unknown until people began to store dried grains and nuts. Later, people preserved food by salting, smoking, and drying. At the beginning of the nineteenth century, other methods of preservation became known.

In 1809 M. Nicholas Appert of Paris, who is known as "the father of canning," developed a special method of food preservation. He heated food and quickly packed it into glass bottles. The bottles were sealed with cork and placed in a kettle of water. He gradually heated the kettle of water for varying lengths of time, depending upon the kind of food being canned.

Appert knew nothing of bacteriology and did not know why the food would keep if treated in this manner. Louis Pasteur, a pioneer in the development of modern bacteriology, discovered the basic cause of food spoilage. Experiments conducted by Pasteur revealed that living micro-organisms such as molds, yeasts, and bacteria were present in the air, in drinking water, in the soil, and on all objects. When these micro-organisms came in contact with food, they caused the food to spoil. The secrect to preventing food spoilage was to kill the micro-organisms (sterilization).

The next step was to find containers that could be sterilized with boiling water. First there were bottles with cork stoppers, sealed with sealing wax. These were followed by glass containers, earthenware crocks, and jugs. Cans of tinplate, sealed with solder, were also an early development. About 1858 glass jars with threaded openings were developed. A metal cap could be screwed onto the jar. A rubber ring placed between the cap and the jar kept the air out. Today foods are canned in glass jars and aluminum cans.

Chapter 4: Prairie Fever

People who have malaria suffer from chills and fever, anemia and enlargement of the spleen. Some people become so sick that if not treated, they may die. The area along the Red River was known to have many mosquitoes in the early days in Texas. People didn't know that the mosquitoes carried the malaria parasite that gave them the disease until this discovery was made in 1898. Even though the cause of malaria was unknown, Quinine from the bark of the chinchona tree found in South America had long been used to treat the disease. Many years ago, some people called this medicine "chill cure."

Chapter 6: Meeting Big Foot Wallace

William Alexander Anderson Wallace (Big Foot Wallace) was born in Lexington, Virginia, April 3, 1817. He went to Texas after the Texas Revolution to avenge his brother Samuel's death at Goliad. While applying for his brother's revolutionary war land grant, he met Sam Houston.

Wallace did many things in his day. He hewed logs for government buildings in Austin, was a Texas Ranger and Indian fighter, and was one of the fortunate members of the Mier expedition who drew white beans. By 1850 Wallace was carrying the mail between San Antonio and El Paso.

Big Foot Wallace died January 7, 1899, and is buried in the State Cemetery at Austin, Texas.

Chapter 10: Choctaw

The Treaty of Dancing Rabbit Creek was signed on September 27, 1830, at Noxubee County, Mississippi, and was ratified February 24, 1831. The Choctaw Indians ceded all their land east of the Mississippi River in this treaty.

There were some important articles in the treaty. The second group of articles concerned federal protection of the Indians in the Indian Territory (now Oklahoma). The United States agreed to protect people in the nation from foreign invasion. No whites would be permitted to enter the nation without the Choctaw government's consent. An Indian Agent would be appointed by the president every four years. All alcoholic beverages were to be banned from the nation.

The General Council adopted the great seal of the Choctaw Nation at Doaksville, Indian Territory, on October 16, 1860.

Chapter 11: Meeting on the Kiamichi

Many intruders were in the Cherokee Nation as whiskey peddlers in the 1850s. In 1853 Agent George Butler let the superintendent of Indian affairs, Thomas S. Drew, know that something had to be done to limit the sale of whiskey on the border of the Nation. Many Cherokee people were doing all they could to stop the sale of liquor. They hoped to keep out the intruders that brought whiskey into the Indian Territory, for it caused much trouble for them. Temperance societies (people who were against the sale of liquor) were organized all over the Cherokee Nation to stop the flow of whiskey. Still, some of the Indian agents did not properly enforce the law.

Problems similar to that of the Cherokees existed throughout the Indian Territory.

Bibliography

Allen, Nelson. "Stepping Out in Big Foot." *San Antonio Express News (Daily Star)*, October 28, 1989.

Brown, George Rothwell. *The Speaker of the House.* Brewer-Warren and Putnam, 1932.

DuVal, John C. *The Adventures of Big Foot Wallace — The Texas Ranger and Hunter.* J. W. Burke & Co., 1870.

Encyclopedia Britannica, 1981 edition.

Fascinating World of Animals. Reader's Digest, 1971.

Fisher, O. C. *Cactus Jack.* Waco: Texian Press, 1982.

Garst, Shannon. *Big Foot Wallace of the Texas Rangers.* New York: Julian Messner, Inc., 1951.

Howard, James H., in collaboration with Willie Lena. *Oklahoma Seminoles Medicines, Magic and Religion.* Norman: University of Oklahoma Press, 1984.

James, Marquis. *Mr. Garner of Texas.* Bobbs Merrill Co., 1939.

———. *The Raven — A Biography of Sam Houston.* Austin: University of Texas Press, 1988.

Liles, Maurine Walpole. *Rebecca of Blossom Prairie.* Austin: Eakin Press, 1990.

McKee, Jesse O., and Jon A. Schlenker. *The Choctaws — Cultural Evolution of a Native American Tribe.* Jackson: University Press of Mississippi, 1980.

Neville, A. W. *The History of Lamar County, Texas.* Paris, Texas: North Texas Publishing Co., 1937.

———. *The Red River Valley, Then and Now.* Paris, Texas: North Texas Publishing Co., 1948.

Patman, Wright. *A History of Post Offices and Communities. First Congressional District of Texas*, 1946.

Pearson, Jim Berry, Ben Procter, Wm. Conroy, and Barbara

Stockley. *Texas — The Land and Its People*. Hendrick-Long Publishers, 1978.

Prettyman, W. S. *Indian Territory — A Frontier Photographic Record*. Selected and edited by Robert E. Cunningham. Norman: University of Oklahoma Press, 1957.

Red River County Historical Society. *Red River Collections*. Clarksville, Texas: 1986.

Sowell, A. J. *Life of Big Foot Wallace*. Facsimile reproduction. Austin: Steck Co. Publishers, 1989.

Standard, The. (Clarksville, Texas.) January 1, 1852. Microfilm, Barker Texas History Center, University of Texas at Austin.

Timmons, Bascom N. *Garner of Texas — A Personal History*. Harper and Bros., 1948.

Walpole, Albert Grayson. *The Walpole Family, A Thousand Years or More*. 1988.

Wardell, Morris L. *A Political History of the Cherokee Nation, 1838 to 1907*. 1938.

Welch, June Rayfield. *People and Places in Texas' Past*. Dallas: GLA Press, 1974.

Also: Census records, wills, marriage records, maps of Red River County, Texas, State of Texas, and Indian Territory.

Walpole/Garner Ancestry

Thomas W. Walpole
b. about 1728
d. between 1793 and 1800
m. Elizabeth Harrison (upon her death, he remarried)
m. Rebecca Harrison
Charles H. Walpole
  b. 10/3/1788 He lived on the family plantation in North Carolina and moved to Tennessee about 1825.
  d. 9/28/1851 He is buried next to John Nance Garner II in Rutherford County, Tennessee.
  m. Francis Clements
  Rebecca H. Walpole
    b. 3/10/1812 on the family plantation in North Carolina
    d. 7/4/1881 in Red River County, Texas
    m. John Nance Garner II 1/3/1833
      b. June 1810
      d. June 10, 1847, in Rutherford County, Tennessee
    William Harrison Garner
      b. 11/1833
      d. 1906 in Paris, Texas
    Francis C. (Kitty) Garner
      b. 3/10/1835 in Tennessee
      d. 8/1/1912 in Red River County, Texas
    Mary Eliza Garner
      b. 1840 in Tennessee
      d. (?)
    Louisa Rebecca Garner
      b. 3/6/1844 in Tennessee
      d. 7/7/1879 buried next to Rebecca in Lamar County on Blossom Prairie
    John Nance Garner III
      b. 1844 in Tennessee
      d. 10/31/1919 in Red River County, Texas
      John Nance Garner IV, former Speaker of the House of Representatives and Vice-President of the U.S.A. under Franklin D. Roosevelt (1933–1941).
        b. 1868 in Red River County, Texas
        d. 1967 in Uvalde, Texas
    Charles B. Garner
      b. 12/26/1847 in Tennessee
      d. 8/14/1898 in Red River County
(Rebecca's children who traveled 700 miles from Tennessee to Red River County, Texas, in a covered wagon in 1851)

LEGEND: b. (born)   d. (died)   m. (married)

123